SOLID GROUND

GODS OF CHAOS MC
BOOK TWO

HONEY PALOMINO

ONE

Lacey

Some dates are more memorable than others.

"So, you're Lacey?" the handsome, middle-aged man across the table from me, asked.

"I'm whoever you want me to be," I replied, smiling sweetly at him.

He chuckled, nodding his head, stretching out his arms and placing his hands behind his head as he leaned back in his chair. An air of confidence exuded from his large frame. Light threads of silver wove through his black hair, his heavy hooded eyelids squinting as he laughed.

"Monty said you were eager to please," he said, his smile, while it might have been charming and playful to any other young woman, was sickening to me.

I didn't reply. Not with words. Instead, I winked at him slyly, a half-smile forming on my red-painted lips as I slipped my stiletto off under the table, and trailed my black-stockinged toe along his ankle. I slipped under the slacks of his Armani suit, slowly inching up his leg. It worked every time.

It shut them up.

I hated hearing them talk. And most of them loved the sound of their voice more than anything else they were paying for. They thought they were so charming. So smart. So entertaining. So fucking *important*.

To me, they were none of that. They were boring on the best nights, and downright abusive on the worst.

I played along. I played the part perfectly - the pretty girl that knew how to pretend you were fascinating during dinner and, even better - how to pretend you had the biggest prick she had ever seen at your hotel room afterwards.

I knew how to follow the rules. Because I knew what happened when I didn't.

After hours of small talk over an outrageously extravagant dinner, my companion paid the check, and we walked down the street that led to his five-star hotel. When he said he wanted to stop at the corner store, I figured he was buying condoms.

But not this guy.

No.

He bought a dozen eggs. And a bottle of wine. Sure, the eggs were odd, but I was trying not to overthink things.

When we got back to his hotel, the first thing he did was open the wine and offer me a glass. I accepted, downing it quickly and asking for more. He refilled my glass as I sat on the sofa. He sat next to me, each of us silently sipping the dry, red wine. It was painfully awkward, and I tried to make small talk again to break the ice.

"So, you live in Seattle?"

"Yes, I do. I'm the CEO of Puget Energy. I've known Monty for two years now. He's a very…efficient…politician." He sipped his wine, and looked over at me.

"Yes, he is," I replied. *He was also a very efficient prick*, I thought to myself. Monty Patterson had been the mayor of Seattle for two years now. He just so happened to be my pimp and owner, also. And he had been for four long years before he even ran for office.

"Does he treat you well?" the man next to me on the bed asked.

"Of course," I lied.

He nodded, staring out through the glass door that led to the balcony of his room and overlooked the bright lights of the sprawling Seattle skyline.

"Do you like eggs?" he asked. He rose to his feet, and I watched him with confusion as he began to undress.

"Eggs? I'm not very hungry…after that dinner we just had and all…" I said. What an odd question to ask, I thought, especially as he began to take off his clothes.

"There's something about them, you know?" he said, as he loosened his tie. "I love their texture. So smooth. So round. So solid. And yet, so fragile. Delicate, even."

"Um, sure, I guess so…" I wasn't sure what he was getting at, but he wasn't paying Monty fifteen grand for me to think.

"More wine, Lacey?" He stood in front of me in nothing but his silk trousers and black dress socks. He was in good shape, I had to give him that. Thick, curly hair covered his muscular chest and the six pack that he was obviously very proud of. The hair tapered down into a thin line that disappeared into his pants.

"Absolutely," I replied. Wine was one of my best friends on nights like these. Hell, it was my best friend every night. It made all the bullshit a little easier to endure. He filled my glass once more before leaving the living area and returning to the kitchen of the suite.

I looked around at the penthouse while I waited. I had a keen eye for nice furnishings, and this hotel had not skimped on their decorating budget.

I was used to nice things by now. Not that I had grown up this way, though. While my mother had desperately longed for a life filled with luxury, it had remained just outside of her reach. Not that she hadn't gone to the dark depths of humanity to obtain it, that's for sure. When you've sold your child to the devil, after a lifetime of using her for your own financial gain, well…you've reached a pretty dark place.

It's not that my mother was evil. She was just stupid, heinously misguided and tragically poor. I had the misfortune of being the one child born to her, and consequently, the only chance she felt she ever had to acquire the lifestyle she had spent her life chasing.

The high life. The good life. The life of luxury.

As soon as I was born, she wasted no time trying to make money off of me. She signed me up with modeling agencies, took me to auditions for commercials for diapers, baby food and baby clothes. And once I could walk, the pageants started. I was barely able to find my way across the stage when she entered me in the first one.

It was the Regal Princess pageant for children ages one to three.

Unfortunately, I won.

And that little taste of victory spurred her on to enter me into every pageant she could find in Oregon, Washington, Utah and California. My entire childhood consisted of being primped, made-up, dressed-up and paraded around in front of a bunch of other equally dysfunctional mothers that lived their own fucked-up fantasies out through their children in some kind of sick competition with each other.

And of course, I went along with it. I was kid. It was all I had ever known. Some of my first memories include her being completely ecstatic about some part I had gotten. I craved approval. I was always that kind of girl. I didn't know anything about rebellion. I didn't know how to say no. It was all I had ever known. Hell, I didn't even know saying 'no' was an option.

If I was being honest with myself, I would say it wasn't an option. If I ever dared complain, my costume was too tight, my shoes were giving me blisters - the quick pinch of her fingernails on the back of my arm would quickly put me right back on track, and I'd suck it up.

Of course, that was when I was younger. As I got older, I knew something wasn't right. While she was entirely concerned with my physical appearance, and coming across as the perfect, loving maternal figure when some one was watching - behind closed doors, it was as if I didn't exist.

Left to my own devices, I could care less if my hair was clean, let alone the dress I was wearing. I was more interested in whether or not she was going to feed me that day or stay locked in her bedroom and forget about that one important task of being a Mom.

She was never a Mom. I don't know what she was. I spent many years trying to figure out why she had me in the first place. She mostly resented me - that is, when she couldn't use me to make a few bucks.

When I got older and stopped winning the pageants, the money dried up. She took it upon herself to find another, more profitable way of using me.

Which brings us right back to this room.

If she hadn't sold me to Monty when I was sixteen, I wouldn't be sitting here on this velvet couch, staring up at a strange man holding a dozen eggs in his hand, and regaling me with their beauty.

"...and the pure whiteness of them is just beautiful, don't you think?" Delicately, he lifted an egg from the carton, holding it up to the light. I was still confused. It was so much easier when they just fucked me, came within twenty seconds, and left me alone in the room for the rest of the night. Apparently, this guy had something else in mind.

"Sure, sure..." I mumbled through the rim of the wine glass. I eyed the bottle on the glass table in front of me, trying to determine if there was going to be enough left to get me to sleep. If this guy kept droning on about eggs, I might not need any help falling asleep at all.

He put the eggs in my lap, and stood in front of me expectantly. Had I missed something? I wasn't being a good listener. I wasn't earning Monty's money very well tonight.

"I'm sorry, Drake, can you tell me what you want me to do with the eggs again?"

He was unbuckling his thin, leather belt, and he let his silk pants fall to the floor. He stepped out of them, and very slowly and carefully, folded them, taking care not to wrinkle the pleats as he placed them on the table in front of me. He smiled as he began talking again and he removed his black boxers.

"Well, if you don't mind, I'd like to play a little game." Standing in front of me with nothing covering his pale white skin, except his pair of knee-high black dress socks, he looked ridiculous.

"A game?" I suppressed a laugh as I watched him walk over and sit on the floor, his back against the wall. He spread his naked legs, his flaccid penis and balls flopping onto the floor like a slab of raw meat.

"Um…" This was new.

"If you could just take those eggs and sit across from me, please?"

"Sure, I guess…" I said. Always the good girl, no matter how fucked up or weird it was. I wanted to say no, throw the eggs at him, one by one, watch the bright yellow yolk run down his perfect body and run out the door, but I knew I wouldn't do that. Monty was very persuasive when it came to my obedience. But hey, maybe that's where this guy was going anyway.

"Oh, wait! Could you take off your dress first, please?"

I groaned inwardly, but I did as he asked, pulling the tight black dress over my shoulders. I stood in front of him wearing only my bra, panties, garter belt, stockings and stilettos. Those fucking uncomfortable stilettos that Monty always insisted I wear. I hated them, it was so hard to find a comfortable pair. Give me a good pair of boots or sneakers and I was happy.

"Good, good," he said, as I sat across from him. "Could you move back a little further? Oh, yes, yes, that's it…"

I scooted back and watched him from across the room. Small beads of sweat formed on his upper lip and his penis began growing between his legs.

"Now, if you could just roll the eggs over to me, one at a time, very slowly…"

Is this guy for real? I thought to myself.

"Roll them?"

"Yes, just put one on the floor…yes, just like that, that's so good…yes, Lacey, oh yes…now just roll it towards me, right between my legs, give it a good gentle, but firm, push…"

I did so, and tried not to look horrified at the same time. I smiled, pretending I was onstage somewhere, pretending the fucking stiletto I was wearing wasn't digging into the back of my ankle. I could do this.

The first egg wobbled around and stopped halfway between us.

"Um…" I mumbled, reaching for it.

"Oh, no! Leave it!" The growing aggressiveness in his voice startled me. "Just use a new egg."

"Oh."

I pulled another egg from the carton, and pushed it harder this time. It went further but still didn't reach him. I was wondering what the hell he was going to do with the egg once it reached him, but I didn't dare ask.

"Try again, Lacey. Harder this time, put some gusto into it! But be careful not to break it."

"Okay, sure," I replied. "Sorry."

"Oh, no, don't be sorry! This is part of the game, don't you see?" he asked. "You are so pretty, Lacey!" His eyes were twinkling and his cock was hard now.

I sighed, picked up a third egg, and sat it on the ground. This time, I pushed even harder, determined to get it across the hardwood floor to him.

It worked. I don't know why I thought he was going to catch it with his hands, but he didn't. Instead, he let the egg hit his cock, and as soon as it did, his eyes rolled back in his head and he shuddered in ecstasy.

You gotta be fucking kidding me, I thought. *He's paying fifteen grand for this? Monty has some seriously fucked up friends.*

"Keep going, Lacey, don't stop, okay?"

I shrugged, picked up another egg, and rolled again. Now that I knew how hard to push the egg, I hit him every time.

If this was some video game, I would have the high score by now, I thought.

Ding! Ding! Ding ding ding!

By the time I had rolled the last egg, he had come all over the floor and was slumped against the wall, a thin line of spittle falling down his chin.

"I…uh…I'm all out of eggs," I said. I had never been so thankful to be out of eggs before.

"Start over," he mumbled, as he stroked his softening cock back to an erection again.

***

A light breeze hit my face as I emerged from the hotel. This had been one of the easier jobs, and yet also the strangest.

Eggs! I thought, shaking my head as I walked down the street. He paid Monty fifteen thousand fucking dollars for me to roll eggs at his cock. For that much money, he could have built a machine to roll the eggs for him.

Rich people were weird. While I enjoyed the luxuries that Monty provided, I definitely didn't consider myself rich. Monty was rich. His 'friends' were rich. I didn't disillusion myself for a minute. I was merely a servant.

A slave, literally.

Sure, I was fed up with it. I was twenty-two now, more than anything I wanted to have a normal life. But this was all I had known. I had never had a normal life, let alone a normal job.

I shook my head as I continued down the street. The apartment Monty had gotten me wasn't far and he would be in there and waiting for me, no doubt having been contacted by Drake to inform him the moment I had left. If he ever recovered from his egg-fueled bliss, that is.

Even if I did try to leave, Monty would find me. Besides, I didn't have the money to go far. There was no doubt in my mind that I wouldn't be able to get away. And I knew that once he did find me, I wouldn't be leaving my apartment for a very, very long time. Monty was adamant that nobody see the bruises he frequently left, so he kept me locked up until they had healed. And on the rare occasions I pissed him off, the bruises tended to linger a little longer.

But that didn't keep me from fantasizing about it.

Which is just what I was doing when the black sedan rolled up next to me, the back window slowly inching down as the driver crawled to a stop next to me.

"Hey," the voice in the back called. I turned to look and saw a man smiling back at me. Rugged and handsome, he waved me over.

Normally, I would have ignored him and kept walking. But there was something about his dark eyes that intrigued me.

What harm would it do to talk to him? I thought. I had never had a real boyfriend. Never been on a real date. Not one that someone hadn't paid for first, and that didn't count.

My curiosity got the best of me, and I strode over to him. I knew I looked good tonight. I had taken extra time with my long blonde hair, and the curls I had so meticulously formed cascaded down my back. My short black dress hugged my curves perfectly, and the those awfully painful, stupid shoes I was wearing perked up my ass nicely.

I leaned down to look in the stranger's window.

He was even more handsome up close. His dark eyes were undeniably sexy, sensual even. He was dressed in an expensive black suit. A red, silk tie. Shiny, Italian leather shoes.

"What's your name, beauty?" he drawled. A Southerner. The one accent that brought me to my knees every time.

"Lacey," I replied. I smiled at him, hoping to somehow charm him quickly so that I could get back home to Monty without being late. I don't know what I was thinking, really. I guess I wasn't, I just wanted to feel something real - for once in my life.

"I'm Ben," he said. My hand was on his door, and he reached up and stroked it lightly as he said his name.

"Would you like to go for a ride with me?" he asked. He smelled amazing, and my eyes trailed down his body, taking in his muscular frame.

Of course I would, I thought.

"I can't," I replied simply. "I have to be somewhere."

"Are you sure?" he asked.

"Yes, sorry," I murmured.

"What if I paid you?" he asked. I sighed. Of course, that's what this was. Why did I ever think someone would be interested in me in any real way?

I stood up.

"You couldn't afford me," I replied, turning to walk away.

"Wait. What if I offered you a thousand dollars?"

I laughed, and continued walking down the street.

"Five thousand?" he asked and I laughed again.

The car began to crawl along beside me. I could feel his eyes on me, and I shook my head.

"What about twenty thousand?" he said.

I stopped short. I looked at my watch. My fantasies of running away had been strong lately, and the offer of twenty thousand dollars paid to me, not Monty, could definitely help with that plan.

Was there time? I thought. Monty was surely waiting up for me. Maybe I could work something out with this guy for later. Maybe I could call Monty and make up an excuse about being late.

"Twenty thousand?" I asked.

"Sure…" he said, shrugging. "No big deal…"

I walked back to the window, leaned in, my low cut dress threatening to spill my breasts out into his car.

"What did you have in mind? I don't have much time."

"Get in," he said. I looked into his eyes once more, trying to decide if I could trust him. He didn't look violent. He didn't look like a murderer. But if there was anything I had learned throughout the years, it was that looks were deceiving.

I stood up, looking up and down the street. I could see the high rise three blocks away. Monty was in there, waiting for me, expecting me. Ready to kick my ass if I showed up late.

But twenty thousand dollars could take me far away from here. If I had that much, I could get so far away that Monty would never find me. I could change my name, my identity. I could start over. I could be a whole different person. Live a whole different life.

"Show me the cash," I said, proud of myself for requiring proof.

He smiled, reached over and pulled a briefcase onto his lap. He opened it. It was filled with perfectly stacked bundles of cash.

As if it had a mind of its own, my hand reached for the door handle and opened it. I slid in beside him, the warm leather seat smooth under my bare legs. I turned to him, and smiled.

"So, Ben," I said, "where are we headed?"

Ben smiled, and reached into his suit pocket.

"Downtown," he said, showing me his bright, shiny badge.

TWO

Riot

"Why don't you ever fuck me anymore?"

I groaned and turned away from the pissed off woman standing in front of me. Ruby was a pistol. Full of neediness, sarcasm and bitterness, she had become a royal pain in my ass. All she wanted to do was fuck, and while I used to be ready as soon as her panties hit the floor, lately, I just couldn't seem to get it up for her.

"I've just got a lot on my mind, Ruby..." I murmured as I walked away. I made it three steps into the Gods of Chaos MC clubhouse before she followed me.

"Riot! Don't just walk away from me like that!"

I stopped and she bumped into my back. As I turned, I felt that familiar anger bubbling up inside. I didn't want to be an asshole. I wasn't heartless like most of the other Gods. I wouldn't dare lay a hand on a woman. And Ruby knew that. Maybe that's why she was so reluctant to get the hint I had been trying to give her the last few weeks.

"Ruby, look. I'm just not feeling it, okay? It's not you..." I said, before I walked away again, leaving her standing alone by the front door. But it was. Maybe if I was really a decent guy, I would have told her the truth. Told her that her constant neediness was a turn off. That the way she flaunted herself around in front of the other Gods just to make me jealous had the opposite effect. That, for some reason, I had decided I just didn't like spending time with her anymore.

I heard her sob behind me, and the sound of her footsteps as she ran out the front door.

It was just as well, I thought. She had been hanging around the clubhouse for the last two months, and I just couldn't give her what she wanted. It was hard enough being in her presence. Fucking her was the last thing on my mind these days.

Truth was, I didn't know anyone I wanted to fuck.

So many women had passed through the clubhouse doors over the years, and I had partaken in my share of them. I had a great time, don't get me wrong. There's nothing like taking two, three or even four women to bed at the same time. I had some great memories.

But I had begun to want more.

Unfortunately, as a member of the Gods of Chaos Motorcycle Club, that was nothing more than a dream. Relationships were for normal people.

We were far from normal. We were the rejects of society. The very definition of rebellion. A gang of misfit criminals.

We didn't 'do' normal.

The only person who had managed to find some semblance of a normal relationship was our President, Ryder. And if he hadn't stumbled upon Grace about to get her teeth kicked in by a pimp on the dirt road leading to our clubhouse, he never would have met someone like her.

Now that Grace had left the police force, and given up her job as an undercover cop, she and Ryder had built a strong life together. They were doing good work together, too - hell, we all were. I was glad Ryder had met Grace - it had given all of us once-worthless Gods a chance to redeem ourselves by doing some good in the world. We had formed an underground railroad of sorts to help the women that needed it the most. It was a perfect marriage of chaos and vigilantism.

Not that we were exactly on the right side of the law. We still performed our job, we just balanced out our karma with saving a few people in the meantime.

That was just the way it went.

We had all given up on normal long ago.

The chaos still existed.

It ruled our lives.

It permeated the very fabric of our souls.

And there wasn't a one of us that could fucking live without it.

THREE

Lacey

"What are you in for, Princess?" The large woman sitting next to me on the hard wooden bench leaned heavily into me, her massive breasts pressing into the goose bumped flesh of my right arm.

It was freezing. I was shivering. If her breath wasn't so offensive, I might have welcomed the warmth of her body. Instead, I leaned away.

I could have gotten up and walked to the other side of the jail cell, but my options were limited. Various women of all shapes, sizes, and mental stability lined the walls, and there were only two other seats available, both of which would have left me sitting next to women that were even more scary than the woman next to me.

She wouldn't have been so bad if she would only stop talking. I was freaking out, and I had been for the last two hours, but I was trying desperately not to show it and keep my cool. The last thing I wanted was to hear this woman's life story.

"It was mistake," I murmured.

"Yeah, that's what they all say," she replied. "So, what, prostitution?"

15

"Yeah, but I'm not…a prostitute. Not like that, anyway…" I replied.

"So what kind of prostitute are you?" she asked, chuckling heartily, her hot, rancid breath hitting the side of my face with full force.

"I'm not a street hooker, this is all a mistake," I replied. Why was I telling her that? I slammed my mouth shut. Monty was already going to kill me, I didn't need to be talking to anyone in here.

"Oh, you're one of those high class bitches, huh? I know your type, I get it," she said, her eyes trailing up and down my body. "You got yourself a sugar daddy, honey? He takes care of you, buys you things, takes you out on the town?"

"Hardly," I scoffed. I couldn't remember the last time Monty took me anywhere that didn't end up rewarding him with either more power or more money. That was all he cared about. I was just a tool to help him achieve those things.

Maybe it was because I was exhausted. Maybe it was because my heels were digging into the back of my ankle. Maybe it was because I was sitting in a goddamned jail cell with a bunch of incredibly scary women, and it was a stark reminder that my life never had been and never would be normal. Whatever it was, it still had the same effect - I started crying. My eyes filled with tears, and as soon as they began spilling down my face, the anger hit me.

Of course, one would never know. I shoved it down to the depths of my heart, just as I always did. Anger, shame, pain, they were all things I couldn't afford to let myself feel. As was sadness. As quickly as the tears began, I wiped them away, took a deep breath, and they were gone.

I was surprised they had even surfaced at all. If I hadn't been sitting in jail, I would have beat myself up about it for days. I granted myself a small bit of forgiveness, and lifted my chin defiantly.

I was strong. I could handle any situation. Monty would be here soon, and although I knew he was going to beat the hell out of me as soon as he got me home, at least I would be out of here before too long.

All I needed to do was focus on the task at hand, and if that meant enduring a conversation with the babbling woman next to me, then fine.

I turned to her, and saw she was staring at me intently.

"You're a strong bitch, huh?"

I sighed. Shrugged.

"How old are you?" she asked.

"Twenty-two."

"You're so young, darling. You've got your whole life ahead of you. You should get yourself an education and leave this life. Whether you got yourself a sugar daddy or a pimp, or whatever you wanna call him, girl, it just ain't worth it."

I sighed again, her words seeping into my brain, even though I tried to push them out.

"That's not really an option for me," I said. I met her eyes, and they pierced my soul. Why was she saying this stuff to me? She had no reason to be nice to me, to even say a word to me.

"Well, now, that's where you're wrong," she said.

"You don't understand…" I said.

"Enlighten me."

"Forget it," I said, turning away. I was being rude, but what use were manners in a place like this? I crossed my arms over my chest, and folded into myself.

"Okay, okay, it's all good," she said, herself turning away and scanning the room before she kept talking. "See that girl right there?" she asked, pointing her chin to a terrifyingly skinny black woman in the corner across from us. She was talking to herself, her hands waving in front of her face.

I nodded.

"That's Sylvia. She's here almost every weekend. She belongs to Mario Sanchez, he's the leader of the Los Gatos street gang. He's been pimping out Sylvia, and a few dozen other women, for years. He gets 'em young. Turns 'em out, gets 'em addicted, most of 'em get pregnant, have crack babies that either die or get taken away before they even get a chance to hold 'em."

I took a deep breath, nodded.

Where the fuck was Monty?

What was taking him so fucking long?

"And over there? You see that girl puking in the bucket?"

A very young girl was bent over, her face pushed into a dirty bucket. She straightened up, and her stringy blonde hair was stuck to her face. She brought a filthy, shaking hand up to push her hair behind her ear and her eyes met mine.

They were dead. I expected anguish. Pain or sadness. But there was nothing there at all. She was a living zombie. I broke her gaze and turned away, keeping my eyes glued to the floor as the woman next to me kept talking.

"That's Misty. She's hooked on heroin. Her step-dad pimped her out to his friends when she was young, and she ran away. She lives on the streets. If you can call that living. All she cares about is how she's going to get her next fix. She doesn't care what she has to do to get it."

"Look, why are you telling me all this?" I asked, the anger bubbling up inside me, threatening to spill out of my eyes in another torrent of unwanted tears.

"Because you're just like them."

"No, I'm not!" I answered, a little too emphatically. Head turned, dozens of eyes landed on me. I shut my mouth and glued my gaze back to the cement floor in front of me. She was more right than she knew.

"Yes, you are, Princess...I can see it in those dead eyes of yours. Here," she said, and she pushed a card into my hand.

"What's this?" I asked. The card was blank, except for a black phone number printed on it. No names, just a number.

"A way out."

"What are you talking about?"

"Sometimes, women don't want out. Women like Sylvia, and Misty. They don't have that burning desire for a better life. Sometimes, they do. Something tells me you want out. Maybe you think you're in too deep, or you can't do it alone. Maybe you need a little help. You call this number, you'll find some help. It's not the cops, I promise you. But they'll help you, no matter what it takes. It's not too late to save yourself."

"Look, I don't know what you're talking about."

"Yes, you do. Just keep the card. When you're ready, you'll call. Tell the lady that answers that the password is 'sanctuary', okay? Don't forget that - 'sanctuary'."

"Look, I —,"

"Lacey Carrington!" I jumped when I heard my name called. The guard was unlocking the cell.

"Lacey Carrington!" He yelled my name again, as I sat there frozen on the bench, holding the card in my hand. My stomach churned. I knew Monty was waiting for me. I stood up slowly and turned back to the woman.

"Who are you?" I asked.

"Just think of me as your guardian angel, darlin'." She winked, and turned away from me. She started talking to the woman on the other side of her.

I nodded, slid the card into my bra, and walked out of the cell, the sharp clap of my stilettos echoing on the concrete.

FOUR

Grace

Ryder's mouth on my neck woke me up. I moaned, pressing my body backwards into him. His arms wrapped around me like a pair of pythons - thick, strong, safe.

His kisses trailed down my neck and along the back of my shoulder. I reached back, gripping his throbbing cock firmly, stroking him up and down until he was groaning through his kisses. His cock felt like velvet in my hand, smooth, firm, ready. I lifted my thigh and he slid into me smoothly.

Moaning together, we pressed into each other, pushing, pulling, each of us fulfilling the need that reared its tempting head every morning. After six months of waking up together, we still couldn't get enough of each other.

Ryder pulled out of me, gently nudging me onto my back and pulling his weight up and on top of me, sliding back into me effortlessly. Our bodies fit together perfectly. The delicious way he filled me up never ceased to amaze me, and my body responded to him in ways I had never experienced before.

Ryder was an expert in bed. He knew when to move slowly and sensuously, he knew how to seductively pull me out of my head and into the pleasures of my body, and then he knew when to wildly and savagely take me over the edge with the full force of his masculinity.

He was perfect. He was solid. He was exactly what I needed in my life, even if I didn't know it six months ago.

His own needs took over as he hammered into me, and I opened my eyes to watch him. It was my favorite part, seeing the ecstasy wash over his face after those last few moments of focused, savage desire.

It made me feel needed.

Wanted.

Loved.

His lustful, passionate thrusting brought us both over the edge and his cock swelled, spilling into me as we came together in a chorus of loud moans that made me thankful that we didn't live at the clubhouse anymore.

Spent, sweaty, and sexy as hell, he collapsed next to me, and pulled me into him. My head rested on his hairy barrel chest, and I sighed with satisfaction.

We lay there quietly, listening to the birds chirping outside of our newly built bedroom, our breathing falling together as the first rays of sunlight streamed through the windows.

Just as I did every morning, I said a little prayer of gratitude to the universe. My life was so different now than it had been before I met Ryder, or, rather, before I came tumbling into Ryder's life, is more like it.

Six months ago, I had been an undercover cop, on the verge of bringing down one of the biggest sex-trafficking rings in the state. But I had been sabotaged. By my own partner. If I had known Judd had ratted me out to the pimp I was trying to take down, I never would have gotten in the car with him. But, if I had never gotten in the car with him, I wouldn't be here with Ryder now.

The pimp took me to a secluded road, beat me, and despite the fact that I had hit my head on a rock and was unconscious, was about to rape me and of course, kill me. But then Ryder showed up. He saved me. Took me back to his clubhouse. Nursed me back to health.

When I woke up, I couldn't remember who I was.

Ryder was a champ through it all. He was my rock. My lighthouse in the stormy sea that followed as I tried to regain my identity. It wasn't easy.

Sometimes, I wished I hadn't remembered at all. All the abuse I suffered at the hands of my family. All the years of pain, the rush of disappointment that washed over me when I realized that I had never had a normal family. I never had a family at all, in the usual sense of the word.

I was a piece of property to be used and abused as my much older, evil siblings and mother had seen fit. If it wasn't for my loving, but clueless, father, I would have turned out a lot more fucked up.

But, I escaped. I grew up, and somehow found the conviction to turn the horrors of my childhood into something productive. I did all I could to help other women escape abusive situations. I became an undercover cop, and I was extremely proud of all the women I had managed to help find a way out of hell over the years.

But then, after that fateful night where I was forced to gun down Judd, something changed. I had already hated being a cop. Now, I hated that I couldn't trust my partner. And in a job like that, you needed people you could trust.

After finding out Judd was part of the very ring we were trying to bring down, I knew I would never trust another person on the force again.

So, I quit.

But I knew I would never be able to leave my work behind. I did the only thing I could - I started something new. With people I knew I could trust.

The Gods of Chaos Motorcycle Club had proven to be the perfect partner.

We called our new organization 'Solid Ground'.

I did most of the day to day work, with a little help from Riot. He was a computer genius, and he always came through for me. When the time came that action was required, I had the full force of the club behind me.

And they were much more efficient, trustworthy, and fearless than any cop I had ever worked with.

I looked up at Ryder, and smiled. I pressed my lips to his, and his kiss was deliciously warm, familiar, gentle.

"Thank you," I whispered, and then kissed him again.

"For what?" he asked, his gorgeous blue eyes twinkling as the sunlight caught them.

"For today," I said.

"We just woke up," he replied.

"I know. And it's already the best day of my life."

FIVE

Riot

"What a piece of shit," Grace mumbled under her breath. She sat next to me, our eyes glued to the computer screen in front of us. I nodded in agreement. It never ceased to amaze me how many douchebags there were out in the world. I shouldn't have been surprised, I know. I was a God, after all.

But even the most perverted, sickest, dirtiest of all the Gods of Chaos MC members would never think of going online to lure young girls away from the safety of their homes.

That act was reserved for the most depraved monsters of all.

I was proud to be a part of Solid Ground. Grace and I had become good friends, and I admired her for everything she had accomplished, and for her fearlessness and willingness to do whatever it took to get the job done. She was unwavering in her focus and there was nothing she wouldn't do to take down one of these monsters.

Sure, she had gone through hell and back to get to this point, but that only made me admire her more.

"Ask him where he lives," she said.

I began typing. Pretending to be a twelve year-old girl wasn't easy, but I had been doing it for a while and it got easier every time. The hard part was controlling my anger as I saw the insanity that came back at me through the screen.

Solid Ground worked in two ways. This was one of them. We 'fished' for online predators and when the time came for a real-life meeting, Grace turned all the information over to the police, and they were the ones waiting for the perpetrators when they showed their disgusting faces.

The other way we worked was definitely more of an underground operation that usually didn't involve the police at all, but was a lot more involved, detailed, and dangerous.

Grace knew people from all walks of life, and she had recruited dozens of people that she called "networkers". These networkers kept their eyes and ears open. Sometimes, they were social workers. Sometimes, they were prostitutes, drug dealers, or other cops. Sometimes, they were the PTA President.

Whoever they were, they were also highly trained to spot women that displayed the behavior of those who were in dangerous situations. They approached those women discretely, passed off as much information as they could, along with the number of a cell phone that only Grace answered, and a secret password.

When that phone rang, it set in motion a sequence of events that didn't stop until we rescued whoever needed saving. So far, Solid Ground had been able to remove four different women from situations that they couldn't get out of alone.

Three of them had been hookers with especially violent and well-connected pimps in three different states. We got them to a safe place, and with the help of some friends of the club, a new identity and a new start away from their old life.

The fourth one was just a kid. She had called Grace in the middle of the night and told her a gruesome tale of all the abuse she had suffered at the hands of her step-father. Surprisingly, that one, while one of the worst stories I had ever heard, was the easiest of all so far. The Gods had roared up to the cookie-cutter suburban house in the middle of the day. Turns out, some monsters aren't so tough and manly when their victims are much bigger than them.

It was so fucking satisfying watching that prick being led away in handcuffs, and the bruises that were scattered on his face and body weren't questioned at all once the cops arrived. Funny how that worked.

"He's in Portland," I said, after the asshole replied.

"Good, he's close," Grace replied.

It was a slow process, drawing them out. Most of these monsters knew exactly what they were doing, and they spent days grooming their victims before they made their move and suggested a face-to-face meeting. My job was to keep up the charade until they broke. If I tried to rush it, they got spooked, and went on in search of their next victim, who was actually a real life twelve year-old.

"Riot, you're doing great. Keep him talking as long as you can. I need to go back to the cabin and make lunch. Holler if he bites."

"Oh, he'll bite. This asshole is already trying to flirt with me," I replied.

"Thanks, Riot," Grace said, as she walked out of the clubhouse. "I'll be back in a bit."

I turned back to the computer.

'What are you wearing?' the pervert asked me.

You're gonna be wearing handcuffs, you fucker, I thought.

"Just a tank top and a short skirt, lol...no biggie," I typed.

"Mmmm...how short?" the prick asked.

I took a swig off my beer, burped, and scratched my beard, settling back into my chair for a long session of disgust.

SIX

Lacey

In the six years I had known Monty, I had never seen him so pissed. Harold, his lawyer, had bailed me out. When I got to the car, Monty was seething. His bodyguard drove us back to my apartment, and stayed in the car as Monty went inside with me.

I had never been arrested before, so I knew Monty would be angry.

I didn't know he would be this angry.

"What the fuck were you thinking, Lacey?" He laid into me as soon as the door closed behind us.

Each blow of the back of his hand whipped my head around so fast I couldn't see straight after the third time. Tangy, metallic blood trickled out of my mouth and down my chin. He pushed me roughly backwards, and I stumbled and fell to the plush, white carpet. The sharp crack of my stiletto breaking pissed me off.

Those were my most comfortable heels, I thought, as he straddled my hips.

"Don't you get enough cock from my clients, you whore?"

More blows rained down on my face, and I lay motionless beneath him as he simultaneously hit me and screamed at me.

He looks like he's gained a few pounds, I thought, a million miles outside of my body already.

"You belong to me, you fucking cunt. And don't you forget it. Paid in full, Lacey."

He stopped hitting me, and grabbed my hair, wrapping my now flat and tangled hair around his fingers and pulling backwards hard and fast.

"You're mine, you fucking understand? I say who you talk to, what you do, and who you fuck! Your job is to obey!" he growled, his grip tightening in my hair.

"And since you didn't obey," he seethed, "you're useless to me now. I can't trust you. And what do you think that means for me, Lacey?"

I said nothing. I knew better. There was nothing I could say that would make him stop.

He reached down with his other hand and ripped my panties from me.

"How could you? After all these years? I trusted you, and you've ruined it all, you stupid fucking whore! I think you need a reminder of just who you fucking belong to before I kill you!" I heard the jingling of his belt buckle and closed my eyes.

Monty stood naked before me, but I kept my eyes closed, just as I always did every other time he raped me. His cold hands ripped my dress from my body, and I lay on the floor below him, wearing nothing but my bra, streaks of blood on my chest, and dozens of fresh bruises that I knew would turn a myriad of colors before magically fading away over the next few days.

He slapped me across the face one more time before he started to mount me.

"You better enjoy this, because it's the last cock you're ever going to get!" he snarled, his fingers wrapping around my throat.

My eyes twitched and throbbed, as I clenched them closed tightly.

And then, as if it had a mind of its own, my knee shot up before he could enter me, swift and hard, snapping up like a rubber band, making contact with his balls with a loud crack. He grunted and fell off of me, and I opened my eyes. His hands cupped his balls as his eyes rolled in the back of his head.

For a split second, I watched him in shock, frozen in time.

Look what you did, Lacey!

I had never fought back before. Something switched inside of me, a strength had bubbled up inside of me that I didn't know was there. I jumped to my feet and moved away from him. My broken stiletto lay on the carpet and in a daze, I reached for it.

Monty moaned, still grabbing his balls with one hand reaching for my ankle with the other. I kicked, freeing myself from his weak grip, but stumbling into the table next to the couch. A glass lamp fell to the ground, shattering and scattering splinters of glass on the carpet around him.

My eyes trailed from the broken heel in my hand and then to Monty, my tormentor for the last six years withering on the floor, and back again to the spiky heel.

Monty's eyes were filled with savage anger and shock that I had finally lashed out. He began to rise to his knees, and I knew he was coming for me.

He's going to kill you, Lacey!

In a rush of movement, I was on him, my fist slicing through the air and stabbing him right in the chest, the stiletto sinking into his flesh smoothly, the force of the blow knocking us both to the ground, as I fell on top of him. Our eyes met and he looked at me with astonishment.

"You fucking cunt!" he gasped.

Blood began bubbling out of his mouth. I pulled the heel out of his chest and sank it right back in, over and over. Huge ribbons of thick, sticky blood spurted from his chest, splattering all over me.

My arm stopped moving. I gasped for breath, sobbing. My heart felt as if it would explode in my chest. I looked down at Monty and cried out.

His blue eyes stared up at me, eerily vacant, hauntingly dark.

Very, very dead.

The strength faded from my body, my consciousness began to weaken, and I laid down beside him, gasping for breath, searching for the one peaceful place that I possessed within me, letting the sweet darkness engulf me as I eventually drifted as far away as my body would let me go.

***

Throbbing.

Pounding, exploding heat.

My hands flew to my head as I tried to stop the pain thrashing through me. The throbbing was deafeningly loud, and it took me a few seconds to realize it was my heart beat.

I shot up, opening my eyes, seeing nothing but darkness. My hands reached down, feeling the familiar carpet below me.

My apartment.

I was safe.

The events of the night before rushed back slowly, as did the pain. It spread through my consciousness and my body with equal speed, planting a deep ball of misery firmly in my gut.

I fell back on the floor, miserable, spent. I wouldn't be able to leave my apartment for days, weeks maybe, depending on the damage Monty had done to my face. I reached up and touched my already swollen cheek, and winced. He had been especially vicious this time.

Oh, how I fucking hated him with all of my soul. No wonder I had gotten in the car with the stupid cop. I was desperate for a way out. A new life.

I sighed, turning over and curling my body into a fetal position. A new life. It was never going to happen.

At least I would have a few days of peace and quiet in my apartment. I might have to deal with Monty, but I wouldn't have to see anyone else.

Monty was funny that way. He didn't mind beating me, but he sure as hell didn't want anyone knowing he did it.

The clock in my living room was the only light in the room, and I was surprised to see it was only four in the morning. It seemed like I had slept for days, but it must have only been hours.

I didn't remember Monty leaving, but come to think of it, I didn't remember much at all. The last thing I could recall was drifting off just as Monty had taken his cock out. I was grateful that was where my memories ended. I had plenty of memories of Monty raping me already, it was a relief to forget one of them.

I outstretched my arms in the darkness, also grateful that I had a home to call my own, that I didn't have to share with another girl. I knew a lot of women didn't even have that. I jumped when my fingers hit cold flesh.

"Monty?" I whispered. I hadn't heard him breathing next to me, and it was so dark, I hadn't noticed him still there. It wasn't like Monty to stay overnight, he usually left me alone after he was done with me.

He didn't stir. Quietly, I stood and walked to the bathroom in the dark. I closed the door, and flipped on the light switch.

I padded over to the toilet and sat down, my head groggy, my limbs stiff, my body shooting pain straight to my brain with every step. I sat down and looked at my hands.

Blood.

My eyes trailed to my arms, my chest, my stomach.

Blood.

My bra.

Soaked in blood.

My thighs, my feet.

Blood.

Slowly, I stood and looked in the mirror over the vanity.

I was covered. Head to toe.

Blood.

Dripping from my hair, under my fingernails, on my eyelids, in my nostrils.

Blood. Way too much blood.

Slowly, I walked out of the bathroom and back into the darkness of the living room.

"Monty?" I whispered again. No answer.

I switched on the light.

The heel of my favorite shoe stuck straight out of Monty's chest, and his dead eyes stared straight up at the ceiling.

I looked down at my blood soaked body and screamed, as everything came rushing back to me.

I ripped the bra from my body, and ran into the bathroom. I threw on the hot water, and scrubbed my skin for what seemed like hours, hysterically crying the whole time.

I wasn't crying because Monty was dead.

I was crying because I was finally free.

I smiled to myself as I washed my hair. It was good he was gone! It was fucking wonderful, in fact! And if this is what it took to get him out of my life, then fuck it! I didn't feel one bit of regret for killing him.

All I needed to do now was get away. And that was going to be the most difficult part of all.

You didn't just kill the Mayor of Seattle and get away with it. Especially a man like Monty. I couldn't just leave, they would never let me get away on my own.

Panic threatened to overwhelm me, but I pushed it away. In the time it took to wash away all the blood, I knew exactly what I was going to do.

I dried off, threw on my robe, and went back into the living room.

Monty hadn't moved.

I looked at my tormentor, laying there motionless, lifeless, worthless…and it was one of the best feelings I had ever had.

I knew freedom was going to taste delicious, but I was shaking with nerves. I wasn't there yet. My plan hinged on one thing - I had only one chance, and I had no choice but to reach out and hope it worked.

I found the card on the floor, under the coffee table near my bra, wrinkled and caked with drops of blood. I grabbed my phone, and with trembling fingers, dialed the only hope in hell that I had of surviving.

When I heard the voice on the other end, I burst out in tears.

"What's the password?" the voice on the other end asked.

"S-s-sanctuary?" I whispered, my voice trembling.

"Hello, dear. My name is Grace. You've reached Solid Ground. Are you in a safe place right now?"

SEVEN

Riot

"I got a call," Grace said. "We don't have much time."

"What do you need?" I asked. She had gathered the Gods together at a decidedly ungodly hour. Doc, our resident doctor, a retired Army medic, sat at the end of the table, sleepily rubbing his eyes, his wild grey curls sticking out in every direction. Slade, my best friend and fighting partner, sat next to me, his eyes bloodshot, no doubt a remnant of last night's partying. As always, Ryder was at the head of the table, with Grace sitting closely on his right.

"In this case, I'm not sure. She's in Seattle, we need to get on the road. I'll figure out a plan on the way. And well…this time, there's a dead body involved."

Slade whistled next to me.

"Well," he replied, "Riot and I can take care of that easily." He was right. This was not unchartered territory. When Ryder had found Grace unconscious and about to be killed on the side of the road leading to our clubhouse, he had killed her attacker. When he got back to the clubhouse, he assigned us with the gruesome task of disposing of the body. It wasn't hard at all. Especially once we saw what kind of shape Grace was in. It was easy to pour the gasoline, strike the match, and watch it burn. In fact, it was almost pleasurable.

"Let's get going. We'll take the van. Bring your weapons, just in case. Leave your cuts behind," Ryder said. We all nodded in agreement, removing our patched and worn leather vests that symbolized our loyalty on the table. "Get your shit together and let's all meet outside in five minutes. It's going to be a long drive."

And it was. We drove the three hours north, watching the sun rise above us as we made our way up the highway to Seattle.

EIGHT

Lacey

I always imagined it would be creepy being in the same room with a dead body. I was right.

After I hung up the phone, I went over and closed Monty's eyes, and then covered him up with a sheet.

"There," I said, standing over him. His foot protruded from the bottom of the sheet, blood splattered across his expensive Italian leather shoe. He would have been mortified.

There was so much blood, I couldn't believe it. How could we both have been so saturated? It was hard to believe I had managed to slay him so violently.

Part of me couldn't believe he was dead. I half-expected him to jump up and start screaming.

Slowly, I reached out and poked his ankle with my fingertip. His flesh was cold, stiff, blue. He hardly moved. I reached down and pulled the sheet over his foot and turned away.

The woman on the phone, Grace, had tried to calm my nerves, but it was no use. My heart was still thumping in my chest. I couldn't stop shaking. I was terrified, nervous, in pain, and yet, I was absolutely beside myself with bliss that Monty was actually dead.

Dead! And at my hands…

Grace instructed me to leave Monty where he was, pack what I could and that 'they' were on the way, without explaining who 'they' were. I knew I was taking a huge gamble entrusting my life with a stranger on the other end of the phone, but the way I saw it, I had no other choice. I knew if I left on my own, I would be hunted down within hours.

Monty's driver was waiting downstairs. He had shown up around dawn. I could see him in the limo from my window.

I knew I couldn't let him see me leave. I hoped like hell this Grace woman had a real plan to help me out of this.

While I waited, I started packing. There wasn't much I wanted to take with me from this life, but I threw a few pairs of jeans, t-shirts, and underwear in a duffel bag, along with a few pairs of tennis shoes. I left behind all my fancy clothes, gladly.

"Good riddance!" I said.

No more sequins. No more makeup. No more of those fucking stiletto heels! As my pile of discarded clothing and possessions grew, I became giddier and giddier.

Now that Monty was covered up, it was a little easier to move around my apartment. I didn't know where I would end up, but I knew without a doubt that anywhere was better than here. Anywhere would be better than the horror I had endured at Monty's evil hands.

Fuck Monty. Fuck my mother, too. I wouldn't have called her for help if my life depended on it, not that I knew how to get ahold of her anyway.

I pulled a box from the back of my closet. I sat down on the soft, plush white carpet, and opened it up. It was all I had left of my past, and as I sat there gazing at it all, I wondered why in the hell I had ever kept these things in the first place.

My first tiny little crown from the Regal Princess pageant. The sash

I had worn when I had won the Miss Young Washington pageant. A trophy I won as Miss Teen Oregon.

I pulled out a photo album, and opened it. A bouquet of flattened, dried-up roses fell out into my lap. My Mother had bought them for me after I won the Miss Teen Oregon pageant. It was the only time she ever bought me flowers, and it was only because she was trying to apologize for something.

I squeezed them in my palms, and let the crumbs fall, sprinkling the lush pile with the discarded ashes of my childhood nightmares.

I flipped open the album, and lost myself in the memories that the pictures brought on. My misery was clear as day. Just by glancing at my eyes, I could see how miserable I was. It was sickening to see the coked-out, tight, fake smile of the woman that was supposed to be taking care of me standing beside me, her arm thrown around me possessively in every picture.

It was all an act for the camera.

By the time I was ten, she spent more of her time backstage getting high with the other stage Moms, or secretly fucking their husbands, and less time fussing over every strand of hair on my head. It was a bittersweet trade-off. Of course, that's when I stopped winning the pageants and auditions and when she really started hating me.

I quickly became nothing but a burden.

For a moment, looking at a picture of the two of us together, the fake smile plastered across both of our faces, I had a fleeting moment of curiosity about her. I often wondered what had become of her. Where she was now. If she had any regrets. Considering how incredibly selfish she was, I doubted it highly.

I sighed, throwing the photo album back in the box, and shoving the box back in the closet.

Fuck all of that!

The past was the past, and now that I was going to be free of Monty's oppressive bullshit, I had no need for nostalgia. Especially nostalgia for a life that never actually existed.

There were no genuinely happy memories for me.

I would just have to start making some. As soon as I got the fuck out of this apartment!

Grace called me again, letting me know they were only an hour away. She told me to pack lightly, leave Monty exactly as he was. I had yet to tell her exactly who Monty was, but I figured I would tell her all that when she arrived.

I instructed her how to get into the building through the employee's entrance, told her where to find the freight elevator, and gave her my apartment number. It was still early, and Monty's driver was still waiting patiently outside.

I don't know exactly what I expected, in fact, I hadn't given too much thought to what kind of help she was bringing, but when they finally showed up, I was stunned.

I opened the door to four of the biggest, most intimidating men I had ever seen. The petite woman standing in front of them would have been dwarfed by their energy, if it weren't for her own starkly commanding presence.

The first thing she did was hug me. I hadn't said a word, not a hello, nothing. She embraced me, and her kindness gently enveloped me, reaching so deep under the hardened shell that I lived in and pulling up all the hidden despair I had stored there, until I was sobbing silently in her arms.

The men stepped around us and into the apartment, shutting the door quietly behind them.

I don't remember much of what happened after that. Grace took me in my bedroom, sitting me down on the bed, holding me, stroking my hair until the tears passed. I heard a lot of muffled talking by the men in the living room and after a few minutes, one of them called for Grace. More talking, a raised voice that turned to whispers, and then they all returned to me, the five of them towering over me as I sat slumped on the bed.

"Lacey, is that Monty Patterson?" Grace asked quietly.

"Yes," I whispered.

"Monty Patterson, the Mayor of Seattle?" she asked.

"Yes," I whispered. The men looked at each other, shaking their heads. "I'm sorry. I guess I should have mentioned that on the phone?"

"Well," Grace replied, "a heads-up would have helped a little, but that's okay. We can handle this."

"We can?" The massive man standing next to her exclaimed.

"Yes, we can." Grace said confidently, hushing him with one pointed look.

"Lacey, this is Ryder," she said, gesturing to the man, who smiled down at me. "And that's Doc, Slade and Riot."

The other three men stepped forward and I finally registered just how different they were from each other.

Doc was wide and round in stature, and his wild grey curls were so unruly they were almost mesmerizing. It was hard to look at anything else, but I forced myself to meet his gaze as he nodded to me.

"Hi, darlin'" he drawled.

Slade was skinny and tall, and he half-smiled at me, his grin crooked and missing a tooth. Somehow, it made him charmingly handsome.

I turned to the last man, Riot, and felt a jolt of electricity as his black eyes locked with mine. I tried to look away, but I was unable to resist the pull of his energy. He was huge. Every inch of his arms were covered in tattoos, and his face was covered in a thick, heavy black beard. His eyes peered at me, mysterious and dark, and yet full of tenderness.

"Everything's going to be okay, Lacey," he said, his voice raspy and deep, laced with concern with a slight layer of anger underneath. "You're safe now. You should let Doc here take a look at you. He's a retired medic, he knows his stuff."

"Okay, th-thank you," I said, suddenly feeling very grateful that I wasn't alone anymore. "But what about Monty?" I asked.

"That guy?" Riot asked, arching an eyebrow, and gesturing to my living room behind him. "Well, Doc's good, but he's not that good. There's no helping Monty. He's pretty fucking dead."

Everyone in the room cracked up laughing. I breathed a sigh of relief, and shook my head.

"I meant, what are we going to do with him?" I asked.

"Oh," Riot said, shrugging. "We'll just leave him right where he is. I'm sure someone will be looking for him."

"His driver is outside in the limo across the street," I said.

"Good to know. We'll go out the way we came in. He'll never see us," Grace said.

"You're gonna have people looking for you, Lacey. I hope you don't have any objections to assuming a brand new identity from here on out?" Ryder asked, his intense stare shooting right through me.

"I couldn't dream of a better gift," I replied, my heart soaring with gratitude.

NINE

Riot

If that fucker wasn't already dead, I'd have killed him. Instead, I could only fantasize about the pleasure I would have received at the familiar impact of my knuckles breaking his nose, the satisfying cracking sound, followed by the gushing blood before he hit the ground.

Unfortunately, I wouldn't get to enjoy that, because Lacey had done a fine job of killing the prick herself.

So far, we only knew bits and pieces of Lacey's story, but I could already tell it was going to be a horror story. She filled us in just a little on the ride back home as she sat between me and Slade.

Doc had cleaned up her wounds before we left. Her face was covered in scratches and red marks that would surely turn to bruises and her left eye was slightly swollen, but she wasn't banged up too badly. Her blonde hair hung in loose waves over her shoulders. She wore a loose fitting black t-shirt, and a pair of jeans that hugged her curvy hips that she had tucked into a pair of black, leather boots. In spite of the redness and swollen flesh, she was absolutely fucking stunning.

The only thing that threw me off was the hardness in her eyes.

Although she had broken down when we first arrived, she had quickly pulled herself together. The firm set of her jaw, the determination in her eyes, and the stiffness of her shoulders, all told me she had endured things most women her age would never know.

Things nobody should see.

I sighed as I listened to her answer Grace's questions.

"How old are you, honey?" Grace asked.

"Twenty-two," she replied.

"You have any family?"

"No. My mother…she…she sold me to Monty when I was sixteen. I haven't seen her since. I don't know where she is," she replied, her voice breaking.

"Jesus," Slade said under his breath, shaking his head.

"I'm so sorry, Lacey," Grace said. She was in the front seat, sitting next to Ryder as he drove us back to the clubhouse.

We had managed to slip away easily. A quick confirmation that Patterson's driver was enthralled in the book he was reading let us drive right past him, with Lacey concealed in the back, without raising any alarms.

"Thank you," Lacey whispered, her voice small and quiet next to me.

"Why don't you try to get some rest, honey?" Grace said to her. "It's about three hours to the safe house."

"Okay, sure," she replied.

"You can put your head on my shoulder, if you want," Slade said. I caught his eye and glared at him, a silent warning for him to remain on his best behavior.

"What?!" he exclaimed, glaring back at me. "We didn't bring any pillows!"

"That would be nice," Lacey replied, gingerly leaning on his bony shoulder, and closing her eyes.

I turned and looked out the window, marveling once again at what my life had become.

Ten years ago, I spent every waking moment in the ring. Boxing was the only thing I cared about and it consumed me with a burning passion that ended up eventually burning all my dreams to the ground.

Sometimes, you can want something so much that it destroys you.

I had started boxing in the Army. I joined up when I was seventeen, lying about my age, wanting to do anything to get away from my alcoholic father. My mother had left us alone together years ago, and I can't say I blamed her. He was impossible to live with. I was finally tired of cleaning up after him, worrying if today was the day I was going to find him dead when I woke up each morning, and trying to get him to eat. I felt guilty about leaving, but if I didn't leave then, I knew I never would. I wanted a life of my own.

At first I was just a cook, but then I saw how they treated the boxers. They were the rock stars of the Army. They got special meals, didn't have to work, and spent all their time training. They even got special living quarters. After a year of breaking my back in the kitchen, I went down to the gym where they trained and started hanging around, just watching on my free time.

Soon, I was itching to get in the ring, and the coach decided to give me a chance. He put me in the ring with a very fast, very sweaty, incredibly strong, well-seasoned guy, but I stood my own, even if he did get a few punches in. I was quick and light on my feet, and I fell in love with it right then and there.

Afterwards, the coach would let me spar every time I showed up, and when I started showing up every night, he told me I should talk to my sergeant about boxing full-time. Surprisingly, my sergeant was receptive, even if the rest of the guys in my barracks were pissed with envy.

Suddenly, I was the golden boy. But I didn't give a shit about any of that. All I wanted to do was fight.

I spent all my waking hours either training or fighting, obsessed with trying to make weight, trying to improve, sparring with bigger and badder guys until I had honed my skills so well that I finally got my first real fight.

That night came and it was like I had finally found my purpose in life. I was strong, clear-headed, practiced and ready. My opponent was a corn-fed Midwestern boy that had been fighting for years. He was a strong opponent, but by the time the first bell sounded, I had tunnel vision. The crowd melted away, my past melted away, and I had only one mission.

I wanted a knock-out. Nothing else would do.

I came out of the corner, dancing and swinging, my enthusiasm only serving to add to the adrenaline pumping through my veins.

He hit me hard right away, and I stumbled, but stayed up, kept my wits. We tangled together, over and over, the ref pushing us away from each other repeatedly, as we tried to get our punches in.

I took a few steps back, and faked him out. I came in strong, with a brutal upper cut, hooking him just under the chin. I hit him hard, loud, the crack jarring me, vibrating pain through my fist and up my arm.

He went down fast, collapsing in a heap.

Hard.

Cold.

Knocked-out.

My hands flew up over my head as I cheered, but I quickly realized something was wrong when the ref called for the medic.

The medic kneeled over him, checked his pulse, shook his head.

He was dead.

I had fucking killed him.

I was fucking devastated.

I was just a kid, killing someone was the last thing I wanted to do. Sure, in the back of my mind, I knew that joining the Army would increase the possibility that I might have to do that very thing. But I wasn't ready. Not yet. And when I saw what it did to this guy's family, his friends, I felt awful for them. It didn't matter that I didn't know them.

I fell into a deep depression, following in my father's footsteps, and quickly turning to the bottle, doing my best to kill myself, too.

It didn't work.

All it did was get me kicked out of the Army, and then I just hit the streets of Portland, hanging with the wrong crowd.

One day, I ran into my childhood friend, Slade, downtown. He told me about the Gods, introduced me, and before I knew it, I was prospecting with Slade.

They became the family I never had.

The family I needed.

A true brotherhood that I never would have found on my own.

They saved my life.

And now, here I was, trying to pay it forward.

TEN

Lacey

The bumping woke me up. I raised my head and looked around, seeing nothing but a bumpy dirt road and tall, towering pine trees on both sides.

"Where are we?" I asked Riot, who was sitting next to me, looking stiff and uncomfortable.

"Our clubhouse," he replied.

"Our?" I asked.

"Yes. The Gods of Chaos MC," Slade answered. He sat next to me, all sprawled out, his arm slung around my shoulder.

I shifted in my seat, inching away from him, but as I moved closer to Riot, Riot moved away from me.

I stiffened, the awkwardness unbearable.

"What's an emcee?" I asked.

"M.C. Stands for motorcycle club," Riot answered, his gaze fixed out the window as he spoke.

"You're a motorcycle gang?" I asked, the high-pitch of my voice startling me. I cleared my throat.

Nobody answered.

What had I gotten myself into?

They sat silently beside me, all of us staring out the windows as the van wound its way down the curvy road. Finally, we pulled up to a run-down cabin, or more accurately - a ramshackle mess.   Dozens of motorcycles were parked along the front.

"Motorcycles," I mumbled under my breath.

"Yep," Slade said. "You ever been on one?"

"Um. No, I can't say that I have," I replied. My mother would never have let me risk a scar by getting on one of those. Besides, it wasn't high-class enough for her. And Monty was far from the biker type.

"Well, you're in for a treat," Slade replied, winking at me. Riot groaned beside me, and I caught him glaring at Slade again. Slade shrugged, slid open the side door of the van, and hopped out.

I stepped out onto the dusty ground and felt the crunch of gravel and dirt beneath my feet. I inhaled deeply, my senses assaulted by the heady scent of pine. No other buildings were to be seen, and not a soul was in sight.

"Everyone's out on a job today," Ryder said, he and Grace appearing beside me as I stood looking around. It was quiet, tranquil.

"You're completely safe here, Lacey," Grace's gentle voice was reassuring. I wasn't sure about the whole motorcycle thing. From everything I had ever heard about bikers, I understood they were just a bunch of outlaws.

You killed Monty, a voice in my head reminded me.

Right.

I'm an outlaw, too.

As if being Monty's prostitute wasn't enough, now he had made me a murderer, too.

I sighed, and turned to Grace. I had to trust them. Every one of them. They were all I had now.

"Thank you," I said.

I had no clue about how to proceed with my life, but I sure as hell hoped they did. Grace and Ryder stood next to each other, strong, unwavering. You could see it in the way they looked at each other, with such respect and regard for each other. Ryder was protective, yet he seemed to hang out in the background, and let Grace call the shots.

"Let's go into the war room, and we can talk," Grace said, taking my hand. "There's a lot to cover."

"Yes…okay," I said, allowing her to lead me inside. I needed that, because I had never felt so lost in my life. I was so used to be people ordering me around, telling me exactly what to wear, what to say, what to do, and who to fuck, that I didn't know anything else.

I had a lot of adapting to do.

We stepped through the threshold, and the floor boards creaked under my feet. I stopped as my eyes adjusted to the darkness. The faint sounds of country music filled the air and a roughly assembled bar lined one wall. A low slung, dirty couch stood along the other wall, with a few chairs and tables scattered around.

"It's usually very crowded here," Riot said. "Enjoy the calm while it lasts."

"Um, okay…" I replied. Grace led me into a side room that held a large table lined with wooden chairs.

"Sit here, sweetheart," she said, pointing to the chair just to the left of the head of the table. I had expected us to talk alone, but Ryder, Doc, Riot and Slade followed us in and settled at the table as well. Ryder took the seat at the head of the table, and Grace sat to his right, directly across from me. They all seemed so comfortable, so at ease, so completely at odds with everything I was feeling.

You killed Monty, that voice rose in my head again.

Yes, okay, I had a reason to be uncomfortable.

"Okay, Lacey," Grace began, "I want to tell you a little bit about me, about us, first."

I nodded, and a hush fell over the table.

"I'm Grace, as you know. I'm a survivor of childhood sexual abuse, at the hands of my own family members. I have devoted my life to helping other survivors. My journey began on the police force, eventually going undercover to bust the countless pimps and sex traffickers that roam the West coast. Unfortunately, I learned the hard way that trusting the cops isn't always your safest option. Along the way, I met Ryder. Actually, I won't mince words. Ryder saved my life. This club saved my life."

She paused, her eyes filling with tears as she spoke, her soft voice the only sound in the room.

"Ryder found me unconscious on the road leading to this clubhouse, the pimp I was planning on busting was about to kill me. I owe my life to Ryder," she said, her eyes landing on him. The love that passed between them was almost palpable. I felt a pang of envy stab my heart. Nobody had ever looked at me like that in my life.

"After all of that, I tried to go back to my life on the force, but I just couldn't do it. Eventually, I quit, and I've found a way to continue doing the work that is so important to me. That's why I started Solid Ground. Now, with the muscle and brains of the Gods behind me, I can rescue women in need, using methods that weren't available to me as a cop."

"I see," I said, nodding.

"How did you get our number, Lacey?" she asked.

"Oh. Well, I went to jail…for a few hours. A woman in the cell gave it to me. I don't know her name. She said she was my guardian angel…" my voice trailed off. What would I have done if I hadn't had been given Grace's phone number?

"Ah. Yeah, that sounds like Alex. She's one of our networkers. She helps spread the word to women who might need our services. She must have seen something in you," Grace replied.

"I don't know," I replied. What could she have seen?

"Well, I'm glad you called. You did the right thing. Now, I have to admit, the fact that we're dealing with the Mayor of Seattle is going to make this whole operation a little more tricky, but as long as you do what we say, everything should run smoothly. But, first, we're going to need to hear every detail of what happened, okay? I know it's going to be difficult to go over, but we have to make sure we know all the facts so we don't miss anything and we know what we're working with, okay, sweetheart?"

"Yeah, sure..." I replied. All of their eyes were on me. "Where should I start?" I asked.

"At the beginning..." Riot said, smiling gently at me. I met his gaze, and the churning ball in my stomach stilled. I took a deep breath and began.

"I'm Lacey Hope Carrington," I began. "My mother changed our name after I was born, because she thought our real last name, Baker, wasn't good enough. She decided on 'Carrington' because she thought it sounded regal and wealthy, because of the Carrington's on Dynasty, you know? Anyway, she grew up dirt poor, and she always wanted more. She had me when she was seventeen, and she decided right away that I was her ticket out of poverty. I guess I was a pretty baby, as pretty as babies can be, that is. I never really thought they were all that spectacular myself." I looked around the table, and for the first time in my life, I let the words that have been floating around in my head for years spill out of me.

"But, anyway, well, she became the stage mom and I became the product. She sold me to whoever would pay her. It started with commercials, print ads, and then she threw me in the pageant circuit. Little Miss anything and everything. Most of the time I won, which only added fuel to her fire. She was hungry for money. She was also hungry to feed her coke habit, which I didn't learn about till much later. One cancels out the other, you know?" I smirked. None of this was funny, but if I didn't laugh, I'd die from all the pain.

"So, she worked me harder. And harder. Until I grew tired of it as I grew up. I was burnt out. I stopped trying to please her so much, and I started losing. She became desperate, trying anything to fix the contests, or bribe the judges. Once, I walked in on her sucking off the entire panel of judges before the Miss Northern California pageant. I won that night, but after that I refused to enter again. The money dried up, and so did my usefulness to her."

"That's fucked up," Riot said, his gaze glued to the table in front of him as he shook his head. I drew from the strength in his voice and continued.

"She met Monty in a hotel bar, late at night, after a fundraiser in the ballroom. He wasn't the mayor yet. She charmed him with tales of her young, beautiful, obedient sixteen year-old daughter, the 'young' part appealing to him the most. He asked to meet me, and then, well, hell…she just flat out sold me to him. He paid her ten grand for me, and I never saw or heard from her again. She just left me there in a downtown Seattle hotel with him, turning me over like an unwanted dog."

"Unfuckingbelievable," Riot whispered, his voice seething with anger.

"Yeah…anyway, Monty made his money back, in spades. He charged his rich friends fifteen grand to spend a few hours alone with me. Most of them had weird fetishes that they wouldn't dare utter to someone in their real life. I was the fantasy girl that they could ask anything of. I protested the first few times, but after Monty beat me, well…let's just say that I learned quickly that going along with whatever his freaky friends wanted was a lot easier than enduring Monty's wrath."

"I am so sorry all of that happened to you, Lacey," Grace said. Her eyes were shining with tears, and mine were bone dry. I was re-telling the horrors of my life, and while a perfect stranger was being deeply affected by my words, I felt nothing. I was dead inside. It was as if I was talking about someone else.

"Listen, it was awful, for sure. But Monty gave me a nice apartment, he bought me clothes, food, paid the bills. He wasn't nice, he was a prick, he tortured me. But most of the guys he sold me to were just middle aged, perverted men. They never laid a finger on me, not violently, I mean. Monty was the angry one, the violent one. And I fucked up. I got tempted by an offer a man on the street gave me, and I got in his car. I knew Monty would be pissed, but I honestly thought, in my naive mind, that I could take this man's money and use it to run away. Turns out, he was a cop, and all he did was give me a trip to jail."

Grace shook her head, and anger rose in her eyes.

"That's when I met your friend, Alex. When she gave me the card. But Monty bailed me out and I was back in my apartment with him within hours. That was last night. He beat me. Hard. And he was about to rape me…but…um," my voice trembled and my hands began shaking as I remembered what I had done. "I don't know…I snapped, I guess. I had never fought back before. But I just couldn't take one more night enduring his cruelty…and I started fighting back. Before I knew it, I was standing over him and stabbing him over and over with my broken shoe. I guess I passed out. Next thing I know, I woke up covered in blood and Monty was dead. I took a shower, and I called you. And here I am."

Riot sat beside me, and the anger pulsed off his body. His fists clenched and unclenched over and over as I told my story. It was unnerving, and yet…the fact that he was so obviously angry at all the shit I had endured was comforting in a very deep and satisfying way.

Nobody had ever protected me from anything in my life. I didn't know what that was supposed to feel like. If this was it, then I liked it.

"Lacey," Grace said, catching my eye. "Listen very carefully to me, okay?"

I nodded.

"All that shit you went through, with your Mom, with Monty, with all those men…none of that was your fault. You didn't deserve any of that. Nobody deserves that. You were a victim. You had no choice but to go along with it, in order to survive. Don't for a second think you did anything wrong. You mother was supposed to protect you, to keep you safe, to nurture you, and she failed miserably. But here's what I've learned as I've gotten older. All that shit that happened to both of us, it only made us stronger. You've survived things that people your age can't even imagine. You're a warrior, Lacey. Remember that. You've gone through hell, and look - you're here now, you're safe, you are finally out of that hell. You've won, Lacey."

The tears were streaming down my face before I could stop them. I nodded, unable to speak. Grace's words penetrated deeply, into my brain, into my heart, and I let them take up residence there. I wanted to remember them. I wanted to feel them. I wanted all of that to be true, as much as everything I had learned about myself wanted to argue against it. I wanted to believe her.

"Everything's going to be alright, Lacey," Riot said, his huge, warm hand softly stroking my back, as he whispered in my ear.

ELEVEN

Riot

It took all my strength not to storm out of the room. It was so hard to sit and listen to Lacey's story and not be overwhelmed with rage. Rage for everything women had to go through, just because they were perceived as the weaker sex, the more attractive sex, the sex that had to endure the horrors of what a man could dish out. They weren't weak at all, not in my eyes.

Nobody deserved to go through that shit, and listening to her story made me want to go and kill everyone who had ever hurt her.

When we first started Solid Ground, I hadn't realized I would be so effected by the stories I heard. But each one was worse than the one before, and Lacey's was absolutely horrific. She never had a fucking chance. It just wasn't fair.

Life wasn't fair, though. I had learned that a long time ago. The hard way.

"This is going to be a very high profile case," Ryder said. We were sitting around the table in the war room, filling Lacey in on what would happen next, after she had finally stopped crying. She was tough, that much was clear. But she was so obviously overwhelmed with the situation she was in now, that she was having trouble keeping her shit together.

I could relate. There was something about killing someone for the first time that unraveled you. Especially if you never expected to be that person. I shook off my own fucked-up past, and listened as Ryder continued talking.

"Every cop in Oregon and Washington are going to be looking for you. We'll keep you hidden here until things die down just a little. We'll get you a new name, a new identity, change your appearance as much as possible, and set you up in a new city with a new life. It's drastic, but this is a drastic situation. The main thing we need to focus on right now is keeping you safe."

"And we can do that," Grace said, picking up when Ryder paused. "All you have to do is lay low and do exactly as we say, Lacey, and even though it might take some time, everything will be okay. In the meantime, you're safe here."

"How do you know?" Lacey asked, looking up at me with such worry in her eyes that my heart swelled with protectiveness.

"Because nobody in their right mind would come snooping around here," I answered. I wanted to throw my arms around her, and carry her off to the safety of my room and lock her away from the fucked up world she had been living in. Unfortunately, cavemen weren't too popular these days, so I restrained myself.

"Okay," she replied, taking a deep breath and jutting her chin out in that way that had quickly become adorable to me. "I've got no choice but to trust you guys. I can't tell you enough how grateful I am to each of you."

God, she was breaking my fucking heart.

"Trust us, darlin'," Slade said, winking at her across the table. "It's our pleasure, and you really couldn't be in a safer place."

If Slade didn't stop winking at her, I was going to knock his face off.

The last thing this poor woman needed was a little fucker like him sniffing around her. I made a mental note to set him straight once I got him alone. The glaring looks I had been giving him all day obviously weren't getting through.

"So, what now?" Lacey asked, turning her attention away from Slade and looking at Grace.

"Now, you relax. We'll take care of everything behind the scenes. There's not much for you to do at all, except enjoy the tranquility of the Tillamook woods and start the slow process of recovering. Make yourself at home here. I'll show you to your room, and you can set your own pace, take it easy. The clubhouse can get a little rowdy at night, but everyone is friendly, and if you need something, just ask. The kitchen is stocked, feel free to help yourself. We all have a big group dinner together every night. I'll keep you posted as we go along, okay? You'll probably be here a week or two."

"Oh. That long. Okay, thank you," Lacey replied, looking like a sad, lost kitten that was trying to act tough. I wished like hell there was something I could do to ease her pain. She was so fucking beautiful, with such a sweet demeanor, I couldn't help but feel tender towards her.

My eyes trailed down her body, pausing at the soft swell of her breasts, and I felt my cock begin to twitch in my pants.

No, I thought. *Stop it.* My confused cock had nothing to do with this. I shifted in my seat, and was thankful when Grace stood up and led Lacey away to show her to her room.

TWELVE

Lacey

"This used to be Ryder's room," Grace said, throwing open the door at the end of the hallway. "After I moved in, we built a little cabin in a meadow just through the woods to the South of here. We can hear you if you holler, we are that close."

Grace was so sweet. It was hard to imagine her as a cop. It was also hard to imagine someone had gone through as much as she had and was still so kind and open-hearted. I had closed my heart down a long time ago. If it had ever even been open in the first place.

Barricades and brick walls. Those were things I imagined every time the pain tried to creep in. Nothing could get through, as long as I stacked the bricks high enough around my heart. My mom, Monty, all those other men, they could do whatever they wanted to my body, but they were locked out of my heart. After awhile, I found I had locked myself out, too.

Grace wasn't like me. She still had access to her heart.

"If you need anything at all, don't hesitate to ask, okay? The bathroom is stocked, feel free to use anything you find." She peered closer to my face, wincing as she saw the bruising. "He got you pretty good there."

"Yeah," I replied. I imagined myself stacking my brick wall higher every time Monty's face appeared in my head. "He got it worse."

"Indeed he did," Grace nodded. "And he got what he deserved." She looked into my eyes. "Lacey, I hope you don't feel one ounce of remorse for what you did. Monty was a monster, what he did to you was unforgivable. You did the only thing you could to defend yourself. If I thought it would be good for you, I'd even encourage you to go to the police with your story. No jury in their right mind would convict you. But, you need more than that. If you had a family you cared about, maybe it would be a different story. But I honestly think the best thing for you is a whole new story, a new life, a new you. Away from the circus that this whole thing is going to stir up."

I nodded.

"You're so right. Thank you, Grace." She hugged me, her warmth once again doing what nobody else seemed to be able to - seeping under the bricks and soothing my soul like a calming stream.

"Just be patient, that's the most important thing, sweetheart," she whispered, as she held me in front of her. "And believe you deserve a new start, Lacey. Because you do."

I nodded, trying hard to let her words sink into the space behind those bricks, to let them touch my heart and heal it just a tiny little bit.

"You must be exhausted." She was right, I was. "There's a plate of fresh fruit, cheese and crackers there, and the bed is freshly made up and ready for you to crawl in it. I'll leave you alone now, you should rest. You need it, trust me. Make sure you eat just a little first, okay? Like I said, dinner is a big event around here, but if you don't feel like joining us, or you want to keep sleeping, that's completely fine. You just let us know. It's all up to you."

It's all up to me, I thought. Her words ran through my head over and over as I drifted off later, warm and safe under the thick quilts and soft

sheets of the lumpiest bed I had ever slept in.
I felt like a queen, and I slept like a baby.

THIRTEEN

Riot

The Gods swarmed around Lacey like vultures. Slade, especially, was pissing me off. He wouldn't quit. I watched from the sidelines as he waited hand and foot on her during dinner.

Since Grace and Ryder had moved into their new cabin, they made it a point to make a big deal out of dinner every night, in an attempt to maintain the sense of family that we were all used to. It had worked. In fact, it had made it us all closer.

But tonight, it was irritating the fuck out of me. I was afraid it might be too much for Lacey, but I had to admit, she was holding her own just fine. She didn't seem to be buying into Slade's bullshit, and I was glad to see it.

Slade's bed was a revolving door, and if he thought Lacey was going to be another notch in his belt, then he was sorely mistaken. I was going to have to take a personal interest in watching out for Lacey, I had already decided. She wasn't going to get too far out of my sight, not if I could help it.

I felt sorry for her, I did. But not in a pathetic way - in a way that made me want to keep her safe. She didn't deserve any more pain. I was going to see to it that she didn't get any. Hell, it was going to be hard as fuck for her to deal with the dirty hand she had already been dealt.

She needed family. The fact that our mission was to send her out into the world as a whole new person with absolutely no family at all was not lost on me. I hated it. So far, I couldn't see any other way. Her mother must have been a fucking monster.

I watched with disgust as Slade touched her arm, towering over her while she tried to take in the scene around her. So far, she had met Cherry and Tiff, the two chicks that had stuck around the God's clubhouse longer than any others. They had a knack for making themselves useful, and finding creative ways of making the various Gods happy. Those ways not excluding sexual favors and cleaning. They didn't seem to mind, most days. Every now and then, Cherry's jealous side reared its head, but she mostly kept it in check.

Grace's presence at the clubhouse had a way of settling everyone down, as much as that was possible for a bunch of misfit outlaws. She did her best to keep out of our club business, and we kept her and the women she rescued safe. It was an interesting arrangement for an ex-cop and a bunch of leather-clad criminals, but it worked.

When I saw Slade slide his hand along the small of Lacey's back, I knew the time had come for me to talk to him. It wasn't that Slade was an asshole, not really. He just didn't know when to keep it in his pants. He was like a dog. He would have fucked anything that moved and had two legs, as long as he liked the way it smelled.

"Hey, brother, you got a minute to talk?" I said, sidling up to him. He was leaning over Lacey and whispering in her ear. He ignored me. I nudged him with my leather boot. He ignored me again. I kicked him in the shin.

"Ow! What the fuck, dude?"

"I said, you got a minute to talk, *brother?*" I glared at him.

"Yeah, yeah, okay…" he mumbled, shuffling out the front door. I followed him, looking back at Lacey briefly. Her eyes trailed after us curiously.

When we got outside, the darkness enveloped us.

"What's so important?" Slade asked, as he lit a cigarette, his eyes squinting at me.

"Look, man, you gotta knock that shit off with Lacey," I said, getting straight to the point.

"What shit?" he asked. I groaned, having no patience for his act of innocence.

"Brother, you know what I'm talking about. All that touching, waiting on her, flirting with her."

Slade took a deep draw off his cigarette before he replied. The smoke and his words escaped from his mouth at the same time, ribboning in the air between us.

"I'm not flirting. I was just being hospitable, brother."

"Yeah, right. I know you, you horny bastard. Just don't get any ideas. Lacey needs her space."

He nodded again, squinting his eyes again as he studied me.

"Maybe you've got a hard on for her yourself, huh?"

I bristled, a sudden surge of anger bubbling up through my chest.

"Shut the fuck up, Slade! I'm just looking out for her, that's all."

A knowing grin spread across his face. I wanted to knock it right off. I clenched my fists at my side, summoning the strength to control myself.

"Lucky girl. She's got both of us looking out for her," he said slyly, winking at me.

I shook my head, and walked back in the clubhouse before I laid him out right there.

I wasn't sure what pissed me off more. The fact that he wasn't taking me seriously, or his accusations of my own intentions.

I stopped in my tracks when my eyes fell on Lacey. She was in the corner of the kitchen, surrounded by Grace, Tiff and Cherry and she was laughing with them. Her eyes were lit up, and the smile across her face was breathtaking. She was so fucking beautiful it hurt. A lump formed in my throat as I watched her. She looked so youthful. I hadn't really seen her smile before, and she appeared as if the worry was falling from her features, revealing the true beauty that was inside of her.

I hadn't realized that I had stopped, or that I was rudely staring at them, my mouth dropped open like an idiot, until all three of them stopped talking and turned my way. I jumped and turned away.

Way to go, Romeo, I thought to myself.

Maybe Slade was right.

Fuck.

"We need to dye your hair tonight, Lacey," I heard Grace say as I walked past them and into the living room.

"Let's do it now," Tiff said. "It'll be fun!"

"Oh. O-o-okay…I've never had anything but blonde hair," Lacey replied.

"Black. Definitely black," Cherry said, as they all disappeared into Lacey's room.

I sat on the couch, trying to think of anything else except the fact that my cock was beginning to throb and come to life in my jeans. Once again, my body was betraying my good intentions.

Hours later, I sat in front of the television, ignoring it, while I was still lost in thought, thinking of boxing, motorcycles, anything at all that could distract me from imagining what Lacey's breasts looked like, when I felt a soft touch on my shoulder. I looked up and there were those beautiful green eyes, gently staring down at me.

"Hey," she said softly. "Can I sit here?"

"Of course," I replied, scooting over. She sat next to me, her body looking so tiny so close to mine.

"Wow," her hair was dyed jet black, blown dry, and hanging in soft, wispy curls around her beautiful face. She was even more stunning than before, if that was even possible. The darkness of her hair brought out her the brightness of her green eyes. "What a big difference!"

"Do you like it?" she asked, her voice shy and quiet.

"It looks great," I said. "It really brings out your eyes, you look...," I paused, my cock coming to life once again, pissing me off... "you look really beautiful."

Her eyes widened, and she smiled.

"Thank you," she replied, her fingers running through her curls.

"Did you get some rest?" I asked.

"Yes, I did. I guess I needed it," she replied.

"Yeah, I bet."

One beat. Two. Three. I hated awkward silences. I was terrible at making conversation. I was more of a show person than a tell person. Four beats. Five. Six.

"You want to go for a walk?" The words fell out of my mouth before I could catch them. I suppressed a groan when she nodded and stood up silently.

"Okay, cool," I said, standing up and following her outside. I didn't have to see them to know that every eye in the clubhouse followed us out that door.

Lacey stood on the porch, staring off into the surrounding woods. It was dark, the only light being the moonlight and the light spilling outside from the clubhouse.

"I've never seen so many stars before," Lacey said, looking up at the clear, black sky.

"Yeah, the deeper you get into the woods, the more you can see. Come on, let's go explore a little," I said, grabbing a flash light from the porch railing.

We walked side by side down the road, the dirt and gravel crunching under our feet, our footsteps echoing up into the towering pine trees overhead. A slight breeze in the air caused them to sway, the soft sound of leaves brushing together whooshing through the air.

"This is so beautiful. You must love living out here."

"I do," I nodded in the darkness.

"I'm used to the city. Glass skyscrapers and sidewalks. I mean, Seattle's beautiful, but I never really got a chance to hang out in the country, you know?"

"Well, now you can. As much as you want. I spend hours in these woods every day, running, working out, just walking. Sometimes, you need a break from the chaos of the clubhouse."

She nodded, lost in thought.

"It doesn't seem so chaotic, to tell you the truth. Everyone was so nice at dinner."

"Yeah, well, they're on their best behavior right now. Grace tries to keep every one in check as much as possible when a new girl arrives."

"Oh." She looked upset.

"What's wrong?"

"I don't want to impose, or get in the way or anything..." her voice trailed off, her eyes darkening with worry.

"Oh, no, don't worry about that!" I replied, trying not to laugh. "I said Grace tries - I didn't say she succeeded. It won't last long, trust me. Before you know it, the beer bottles will be flying and the rock music will be blaring."

She smiled, and I watched the transformation with fascination. She was gorgeous, no doubt, but when she smiled, it was like someone turned a light on.

"Okay, cool. I'm pretty easy going, I can take it." She jutted her chin out again. It was absolutely killing me it was so fucking adorable, and it took all my strength not to reach out and touch her face. Warmth spread through my limbs like wildfire, and my cock sprang to life again in my pants.

"Come on, I want to show you something," I said, turning on the flashlight and taking her hand in mine to lead her into the forest. It was an easy, natural gesture and yet I couldn't help but notice how perfectly our hands fit together.

66

We turned off the road and stepped into the darkness of the trees. We followed a small trail I had beat into the ground over the years. The trees formed a quiet hush, and the sounds of the forest filled our ears - a symphony of crickets, frogs, and all the other creatures that shared this land with us.

Silently, I led her deeper into the woods. Fallen pine needles crunched underfoot as we made our way down the trail. After a few moments, the sound of rushing water filled the air.

"There's a creek just ahead," I told her. The awkward silence had fallen away.

We broke through the trees, turned a corner and the creek appeared in front of us. We stopped to take in the beauty of the water rushing over the rocks, the spectacular vision bathed in bright moonlight. I turned off the flashlight, and we stood in the quiet darkness.

Lacey's eyes were glued to the breathtaking sight of the lush, Oregon beauty, the creek rushing over boulders, foaming into white bubbles, and my eyes were glued to her face.

The moonlight spilled over her features, her eyes reflecting the shimmering water in front of us before she turned them up to me, catching me staring at her. Softly, she smiled as she held my gaze. I reached my hand out, caressing her face tenderly.

"You're a beautiful girl, Lacey," I whispered, daring to break the spell I had fallen under by speaking.

She brought her hand up, putting it over mine, and pressing it into her cheek as she smiled up at me.

"You're sweet. But I'm not at my best right now, I must admit," she said, gingerly touching her bruised cheek with her other hand.

"I wasn't talking about your face. I was talking about you," I replied, pulling my hand away and taking hers in mine again. "Come on, let's keep going."

We followed the trail along the creek, the moonlight lighting our way as I kept the flashlight in my pocket. The elevation began to increase, and we continued up the trail, climbing up the hill, until we couldn't go any further. I stopped Lacey before we turned a corner.

"Okay, wait. Close your eyes."

"Close my eyes?"

"Yep. It's worth it, I promise."

"Okay," she said, taking a deep breath and closing her eyes. "Don't lead me over any cliffs."

"You're safe with me," I said, feeling that familiar wave of protectiveness wash over me.

I grabbed her hand again and led her around the corner. The blast of the mist hit our faces and her eyes flew open. She squealed in delight.

"Wow!" Her gaze trailed up the massive waterfall in front of us, the force of the water falling and plunging into the naturally formed pool below. The pool fed the creek, narrowing at the edges as it swept through the forest, like a rushing, bubbling snake.

"This is my favorite spot," I said, as she pulled away from me and ran to the end of the trail, as close as she could get to the waterfall without actually jumping in the pool.

"It's amazing!" She turned her face up to catch the mist, and when she turned back to me, she was smiling.

She's happy, I thought. *Her life is just beginning. She's finally free.*
Her smile faded as she met my eyes.

"What's wrong?" she asked, walking back to me.

"Nothing, why?" *She's probably thinking you're going to attack her you idiot.* I couldn't stop staring at her, and I needed to pull it together.

"You just looked so...oh, nevermind," she replied. "Thank you for bringing me here. I love it!"

"My pleasure. I spend a lot of time here, but I don't mind sharing."

"Well, that's good," she said. A strand of hair fell in her face, little droplets of mist covering her head and shining like little bubbles in the moonlight. I reached down and pushed the strand behind her ear, and to my surprise, she stood up on her toes and brushed her lips across mine casually.

Fire shot through me as her lips touched mine and my body responded without consulting my brain at all. I pulled her into my arms, my lips crashing down on hers and kissing her with all the desire I had been restraining since the first moment I stepped out of the clubhouse doors with her. Her lips were soft, warm, inviting and we melted together, our lips working together sensuously.

She whimpered slightly, and I regained some semblance of rational thought. I pushed her away as quickly as I had pulled her in.

You're like a fucking bull in a china shop.

"I'm so sorry," I said, my voice gruff with desire, my cock throbbing hotly between us. "I shouldn't have done that."

She looked up at me, her eyes filled with confusion and pain and I felt like the biggest asshole ever.

What the fuck was wrong with me?

"We should get back," I said, wanting to kick myself.

"Um, okay, sure." She sounded sad, and it was all my fault. Only moments ago she had been looking up at a beautiful force of nature, looking happier than I had seen her so far, and I had gone and ruined the whole fucking thing.

I grabbed her hand, and led her back the way we came. She stopped behind me, and I turned.

"What's that?" she asked, gesturing through the trees.

I followed her gaze and saw my boxing bag hanging from the tree.

"That's mine. Like I said, I spend a lot of time here."

"You're a boxer?"

"Nah, not anymore. I used to be, though."

"Oh. I see. Why don't you box anymore?"

Good question. *Because I killed a man.* But I couldn't say that to her - not here, not now.

"Come here," I said, an idea forming in my head. I led her over to the clearing where I had spent many hours alone and pounding my frustrations into this bag. It surprised me sometimes that it hadn't broken off, as much as I had punched the fucking thing.

"You ever punched a bag before?" I asked.

She laughed, shaking her head.

"No, never."

"Wanna try?" I asked. This was better. Instead of kissing her, I needed to be teaching her to protect herself. I needed to focus on the situation at hand, and ignore the way my body was reacting to her. I was a man, for fuck's sake, not a hormonal teenaged boy.

"Uh…really? Okay, sure."

I put the flashlight on the ground, pointed it at the bag and reached up to pull my gloves from the top of the bag. I slipped them over her hands, securing them tightly around her wrists.

"They might be a little big," I said.

"A *little* big?" she giggled. "Your hands are huge!"

"Yeah, well, I'm a big guy, I guess."

"So, what do I do? Just punch?" she asked.

"Well, first let's work on your stance." I stood with one front in front of the other, slightly turned, my fists raised up and covering the front of my face.

"Stand like this."

She tried to copy me but it was all wrong. Her hips were going in the wrong direction.

"No, no…here, let me help you." I walked around behind her, my hands landing on her hips, my cock swelling once more, a stark reminder of exactly what I was supposed to be ignoring. I pushed her hips, the curve of them sliding under my palms. I positioned her correctly, then reluctantly pulled my hands away. I reached up, raising her gloved fists up higher.

"That's it, good. Now, remember that. You gotta keep your hands up to protect your face, okay? You start like that every time."

"Okay," she whispered.

"Now, practice shifting your weight from one foot to the other. Kind of like you're dancing. Like this," I shifted back and forth a few times to show her.

She imitated me, and I smiled at her awkwardness.

"A little lighter on your feet. Drop your shoulders, relax a little," I said, pushing her shoulders down. "Good, that's it."

"Now what? I just punch?"

"No, there's a certain finesse to it." I ran my hand along her arm as I extended it, her skin feeling like velvet under the roughness of my fingertips. "Keep one hand up to protect your face, and punch with the other. Let your fist turn down as you approach the bag. When you make contact, your arm should be extended straight out."

She landed a few punches on the bag, trying to dance around at the same time. She looked at me, confusion filling her eyes.

"It takes some practice," I said, smiling at her encouragingly. "You'll get it."

"I like it, though," she asked, holding her hands out as I unwrapped the ties and pulled the gloves off of her. "Will you teach me more?"

"Hell yeah, I will!" I exclaimed, a little too enthusiastically. "We've got lots of time to kill, so I'll give you lessons every day, if you want."

Her eyes shined up at me, the easiness returning between us. I breathed a sigh of relief.

"I'd like that," she said, smiling back at me.

A sudden swoosh sounded overhead and I turned my head up to find myself looking into a pair of familiar yellow eyes.

"What is that!?" Lacey jumped away and screamed.

"Oh, don't be afraid. That's Oliver."

"Oliver?" she asked, staring up at the owl sitting on a branch of the tree that my bag was hanging from.

"Yeah, he hangs out around the clubhouse a lot. Ryder swears he's known him for years, but we don't really believe him. Lately, he's been bugging me a lot."

Another swoosh of the wind, and another owl landed on the branch, perching beside him.

"Oh, my goodness!"

"And that's Olivia. Oliver showed up with her a few months ago, and I haven't seen one without the other since then. I guess they're a couple now."

"Oh, wow, that is so adorable!" Lacey exclaimed.

"I can't argue with that. They're harmless, unless you happen to be a crow, and they don't do much except show up when you want to be alone and stare at you. Little bastards," I replied.

"I love them!" she said, staring up at them. "I've never seen an owl in real life before. Or a waterfall."

"No?" I said. "Well, stick with me, kid, I'll show you things." I winked at her, remembering the feel of her lips on mine, wanting nothing more than to kiss her again.

"I think I will," she said, threading her fingers with mine as we walked back down the trail and back to the clubhouse.

FOURTEEN

Lacey

So that was what it felt like.

To hold a guy's hand. To voluntarily kiss someone. To see that look of desire in their eyes when they looked at you.

For someone who had gone through so much, done so much sexually, or rather had so much done to her, I felt like a virgin.

I had never had a boyfriend, gone on a date, nothing of the sort. Mom had kept me sheltered, home-schooled me, which, in reality, consisted of spending hours painting my nails, experimenting with clothes and make-up to make me look older, or at least meeting some exaggerated measure of the perfect image she had of me in her head.

Her idea of education consisted of me sitting at the kitchen table and reading whatever etiquette book she seemed to think was appropriate. Luckily, I liked to read, and I soaked up every bit of knowledge I could find in those books.

Socializing wasn't high on her priorities list, to say the least. I never had a chance to meet boys my age, because I wasn't around them. I was a virgin when she sold me to Monty. He quickly remedied that, but it was never something I wanted, and certainly never pleasurable.

As soon as Riot grabbed my hand, that was all I could think about. I had never had my hand held. Not even by one of Monty's friends. And I hadn't even realized it until that very moment.

I was in awe that a gesture as simple as a handsome man's hand in mine could barrel through me with such force that it would leave me speechless. A yearning flooded over me as Riot led me through the woods. A yearning for everything I missed, everything I was deprived of, all the normal parts of growing up and experiencing life.

Such simple things.

A warm, comforting hand in mine. A quiet walk through the woods at night. A rushing creek bathed in moonlight.

I had missed so much. There must be things out there I don't even know I've missed.

When I saw the waterfall, I was overcome with emotion. A pure, bliss-filled bubble of joy swelled inside me and everything finally dawned on me.

I was free now. I could do these things. All the things I had missed out on, they could be mine now.

Riot stood in front of me, and I watched him in awe. He looked wild and savage amongst all the raw natural beauty surrounding us. Little droplets of mist clung to his beard, and I smiled. Something about this man filled me with so many different emotions, things I had never let myself feel before, things that the barricades I had built up seemed to be useless against.

And, for once in my life, I desperately wanted to feel those things. They didn't hurt. They were amazing! Tenderness, protectiveness, happiness, and what? Lust? I couldn't ignore the warmth that spread from my limbs to my loins. That was new, too.

It felt as if my body was coming alive, as if my life was slowly expanding around me, as if I was awakening from some deep slumber and had finally woken up to the sunlight.

Without thinking of anything but how grateful I was, my lips, eager for something new themselves, brushed against Riot's mouth.

I didn't think any further than that, but the kiss that he laid on me almost brought me to my knees. I whimpered, grateful he was holding me up with his muscular arms that he had so deliciously wrapped around me, when he abruptly let me go.

I didn't know what to think. Had I done something wrong? I had wanted it. Fuck, I had loved it. The electricity shot through me like a rocket as he kissed me, burning every inch of my body, shimmering inside me for long after he pulled away.

The entire walk back to the clubhouse, I was trying to figure out how I could get him to do it again.

***

"Police aren't releasing any details, but it appears the Mayor was slain in the luxury condominium skyrise, the Escala, in East Seattle. It's not clear at this time who owns the condo, but police have released a photo and a name of a person of interest...."

Riot and I walked back into the clubhouse to see a group of brothers, along with Cherry, Tiff and Grace crowded around the television.

"Shit," Ryder said, standing to Grace's left.

"What's going on?" Riot asked.

The crowd parted slightly, all eyes landed on me as they turned my way slowly. I gasped as I saw a photo of my own face staring back at me from the television.

"Police are searching for Lacey Carrington. Ms. Carrington is not being called a suspect, the police say they just want to ask her some questions. Authorities have not revealed Ms. Carrington's relationship to the Mayor or how she is involved in the case, as of yet."

"Oh, fuck." I sank to the couch, my eyes glued to the screen.

"Don't be alarmed, Lacey," Grace said, sitting down next to me and taking my hand. "We knew this was going to happen. You're safe here, I promise."

I nodded silently.

"Police haven't released any details on the manner of death of Mayor Patterson. The President of the Council, Ron Green, will take over all mayoral duties for the time being." The blonde, perky reporter was holding a microphone that was almost as big as her face, and he eyes were as sharp as a hawks. "We'll be updating you as more information comes in. I'm Diana Trudeau, with KATU news, Portland."

Riot turned off the television and I felt everyone's eyes on me again. I felt like I was going to be sick. I knew this was going to happen, but the reality of it all was just too overwhelming.

"How can you be so sure they won't find me?" I asked Grace again. I turned to look at her, and was comforted by the confidence in her eyes.

"Because that's what we do, Lacey. And we take our job very seriously," she replied.

I nodded, wanting so desperately to believe her, but the creeping doubt inched deeper into my soul.

You killed Monty, that silent voice reminded me.

"I hope you're right," I said. "I'm going to get some sleep now. I'm so exhausted."

"Of course," Grace said gently. "Let us know if you need anything."

I stood up, avoiding all the eyes that were turned my way, especially Riot's.

I knew if I looked at him again, I would either spontaneously kiss him again, or more likely, burst out crying.

And that wasn't me.

I pushed all the thoughts away, and pushed the pain as deep as it would go inside me, and walked to my room alone.

FIFTEEN

Riot

Goddamn, it hurt to see her like that. She looked like she had seen a ghost by the time she finished watching that newscast, and who wouldn't, with their face plastered all over the TV like that?

She had gone through hell, and it wasn't over, not by a long shot. I knew what starting over felt like, but not when you were forced to assume a new identity all alone.

All of us Gods had gone through some sort of hell, otherwise we wouldn't be here. We'd be suited up in a corner office or something. Instead, we were suited up in leather and tattoos, and the constant smell of booze and weed was our cologne. But the thing that kept us all sane was that, at the very least, we had each other. It was a brotherhood of misfits, and I was thankful to be a part of it.

But it just made me feel that much worse that we would soon be sending Lacey off into the world by herself. Sure, Grace had all sorts of support networks in place, but it wasn't the same as every day companionship.

After the usual partying had died down, hours after Lacey had gone to her room, I drunkenly retreated to my own room, refusing Slade's constant provoking and prodding as he tried to goad me into fighting him again. I had no desire to do that tonight, even though it often made me feel better to pummel his smug face into submission.

But not tonight, no. I laid in bed, my mind swimming from the intoxicating effects of the whiskey I had consumed, but even more so, the lips I had consumed earlier. The pain in Lacey's eyes afterwards haunted me for hours as I tossed and turned, unable to get to sleep, the liquor failing miserably in doing its job.

Finally, I got up and rolled a joint. I walked out to the porch for some fresh air, and lit it. Right away, the big swoosh of white wings caught my eye and I turned to the left to see Oliver and Olivia sitting there blinking their big yellow eyes at me.

"Hey there. You two can't sleep either?" I laughed at my own joke. "I guess this is lunch time for you."

I wouldn't admit it to anyone, but I loved these two owls. Many a night they kept me company - either here or at the river while I worked out. I was glad when Olivia starting showing up with Oliver. I was beginning to worry about the little bastard, and it was nice to see he had found a mate.

"Shouldn't you two be out hunting for squirrels or torturing crows or something?" I asked them.

They blinked at me silently, the slight breeze blowing the edges of their feathers lightly. Oliver puffed up, his white wings raising slightly behind him as he began his usual nightly song. It was a deep cooing sound, the who-who-whoing at the end always louder than the beginning. I loved it and when Olivia joined in with him, I smiled.

"You two should have your own Broadway musical or something." I inhaled deeply, the thick smoke doing its job of relaxing me. I looked out at the trees swaying in the wind above me. I loved it here - this clubhouse, my brothers. I had even grown to love Grace and the work I did with her. But damn, if it wasn't a hard existence.

Sometimes, I wondered where I would be if I hadn't killed that guy in the ring. If I had just stayed on the path I had so methodically laid out for myself when I was younger. If I would have found a wife, had a family, a dog or two.

I sighed, letting all the frustrations slide away into the night. I was here now. No sense in wasting time wondering 'what if'. I had to accept my life as it was now, and all the twists and turns along the way that led me here.

They say all that stuff only serves to make you stronger, but seems to me it's only made me tired and weary and skeptical about life in general. And if I weren't any of those things, then maybe I wouldn't feel like such a dick for letting my thoughts about Lacey progress to anything except wanting to help her. But I did. I felt like the biggest asshole in the world.

All these fantasies that I couldn't shake, of wanting to kiss her again, to touch her, to press her naked skin against me and show her how a real man makes love, with nothing but his woman's pleasure on his mind…she didn't need those things from me, I knew that, but damn if I didn't want to give them to her anyway.

She needed a friend. Not another fucking asshole to want her for just her body.

Lost in thought, I didn't hear the door open behind me. Oliver and Olivia didn't seem to feel the need to warn me, either, so when I felt a soft hand on my shoulder, I jumped ten feet in the air.

"I'm so sorry!" I turned to see Lacey's eyes, the eyes that had been haunting me all fucking night, staring at me.

"That's cool, that's cool," I said, trying to brush it off and regain some sense of composure. "I just didn't hear you."

"I couldn't sleep," she said.

"Me, either. Here have a seat," I said, sitting back down on the porch steps.

She sat down slowly, her gaze turning to the owls.

"They're back," she said.

"Yeah, I guess they don't have anything better to do than hang out with a bunch of derelicts."

"Maybe they like you," she said.

I scoffed.

"Maybe. And maybe they're crazy."

"I like you." She said it so quietly, I almost didn't hear her. My heart skipped a beat, and I remembered what I had just been thinking about.

"I like you, too, Lacey," I looked in her gorgeous eyes, trying not to lose my mind. "Listen, I owe you a huge apology."

"For what?" she asked.

"For kissing you earlier...I shouldn't have done that. I know the last thing you need is some asshole all over you like that. It won't happen again, I promise." That last sentence seemed to stab me right in the gut as the words formed on my lips.

She didn't reply for a while, her eyes full of confusion and sadness. As if I couldn't feel even worse.

"But," she finally said, "*I* kissed *you*. I've never done that before."

"What do you mean?"

"I've never kissed anyone before. Not you know...willingly...like that. And that's what I was thinking at the time. Your hand felt so nice in mine. And I'd never done that before, either," she shifted her eyes down shyly. "There's a lot I haven't done. I never had a boyfriend, or a normal life. I've never gone on a real date, let alone kissed someone that I wanted to. I missed so much, Riot. And so that's why I kissed you. I wanted to know what it felt like."

"Oh."

"Yeah," she said, looking at me again, a smile spreading across her face.

"So? What did you think?" I asked, suddenly becoming aware of the warmth of her body pressed against mine. The steps were narrow and we were squeezed between the railings.

"I liked it," she said. "A lot."

Her eyes stayed locked with mine. I nodded silently, and watched as she licked her luscious pink lips, her eyes darting down to my lips and then back up at my eyes. The universal 'kiss me' sign.

Fuck it, I thought, throwing all caution to the wind and reaching down to lift her chin and kiss her again, gently this time, without all the unruly passion of earlier, I brushed my lips against hers, cradling her face in my hands as her mouth opened to mine welcomingly.

She softened under my touch, her lips yielding, kissing me back just as softly, slowly, and gently. Time stopped around us, the owls flew away, and the trees gently swayed overhead, the moon shining her bright light down on us. I pulled her into my arms, kissing her deeper but still gently, until she was whimpering in my arms.

My cock throbbed between us, but I knew, without a doubt, this was no time to go there. I willed myself to ignore it. I had to go slow, even if I probably shouldn't be 'going' at all.

But fuck, if kissing her wasn't the most enjoyable thing I had done in years. I was determined not to let my brain, or my impatient cock, get ahead of me.

SIXTEEN

Lacey

I woke up to the sound of a woodpecker knocking on a tree outside my window. The misty morning sunlight streamed in the windows and I stretched my arms over my head. A smile was already spread across my face, and I could still feel Riot's kisses on my swollen lips.

We had kissed for hours on the steps last night. It had been absolutely magical. I had never felt anything like that before, and I had gotten lost in the tenderness of his touch.

How could such a gruff bear of a man be so gentle? It was an attractive contrast, I had to admit. He was so tall, so broad, his beard and tattoos and the sheer size of him, just screamed masculinity and intimidation. And yet, he was nothing like that. He was kind, gentle, and sexy as hell. And, apparently, as indicated by the way he kissed me by the creek, he was suppressing a fiery passion that he had somehow managed to control while we were on the porch.

Part of me was wishing he would unleash that fury on me again, and take me to his room, but he hadn't. He had been nothing but tender and sweet. That was just fine, though.

We had plenty of time. And if I had any say in it, I would find a way to pull that out of him again. It had felt amazing, knowing someone wanted me like that. And I wanted a lot more of it.

I showered, dressed and went out into the kitchen. I was starved, and so thankful when the smell of bacon assaulted my senses.

Riot, Doc and Ryder were sitting at the kitchen table while Cherry loaded plates with eggs, bacon and biscuits.

"Good morning!" I said to everyone and no one in particular, all at the same time. Riot caught my eye, nodded and winked at me, and I felt a twinge of excitement shoot through me.

"Hi, there, Lacey darlin'! I hope you're hungry, there's enough bacon here to feed an army!" Cherry said.

"I'm starved! Thank you!" I replied gratefully.

"How'd you sleep?" Riot asked, a twinkle of mischievousness in his eye, as if we had a shared secret.

"Well, it took me a little while to actually get to sleep, but once I did, I slept like a baby." I smiled warmly at him. I saw Slade and Doc look at each other suspiciously, but Riot ignored them, so I did, too.

Cherry poured me a cup of coffee, and I sat at the table with the Gods. As soon as she put the food on the table, they dug in like ravenous bears. I tried not to laugh, but it was so good to see them eat like real men. I had never been around men like this, and it was such a refreshing change from Monty and his friends, with their feminine, smooth, businessmen hands and their bird-like diets.

I ate with a newly found gusto myself. Now that Monty wasn't monitoring every morsel of food that went in my mouth, I had found I liked the feeling of being stuffed so full of food that my belly protruded a little. It felt good not to have to think about pleasing Monty.

You killed Monty, that voice returned. But it was quieter this time, and instead of feeling a thick lump in my throat at the reminder of what I had done, I tasted that sweet taste of freedom again. My heart fluttered with happiness as I stared across the table at my rescuers, at Riot, and I was overcome with a surge of gratitude.

"Hey guys, I just wanted to thank you all again...for everything," I said, as Cherry removed our plates. "I can't tell you how grateful I am. I don't know what I would have done..." My eyes filled with tears as my voice trailed off.

"You're welcome, Lacey," Ryder said. "We're happy to help. Everything's coming along just fine so far. We should have you out of here and off to starting your new life before too long."

"You guys are too wonderful. I owe you."

"You don't owe us a thing," Riot said, smiling across the table at me.

"Well," I replied, "someday, somehow, I'll repay the favor."

"Well, you don't worry about that. Right now, you just need to concentrate on recovering and enjoying the, well...the somewhat...peace and quiet here, until it's safe for you to leave."

"I will, thank you," I said.

"So, how about another boxing lesson today?" Riot said. Ryder and Doc looked at him in questioningly. "We walked down to the creek yesterday and she saw my bag," he explained, shrugging.

"I'd love that!" I replied, a little too enthusiastically. I welcomed another opportunity to spend time with Riot alone.

"Okay, cool, we can go as soon as you're ready," he said. He turned to Ryder. "Unless you need me for something this morning?"

"Nope." Ryder was a man of few words, but his eyes spoke volumes as he looked at Riot. A silent warning passed between them, and Riot nodded as we stood up and walked outside together.

SEVENTEEN

Riot

My knuckles cracked as I made contact with Slade's jaw. He had been pestering me for days for another round, and after spending hours in close contact with Lacey alone in the woods while I was teaching her to punch the bag, I needed desperately to work out some physical frustrations. My cock had throbbed painfully all day and I was proud that I had been able to control myself. It was getting harder and harder to continue my gentlemanly ways around her.

She was opening up now, the hardness now just a faint flicker in her eyes, as she let her personality slowly emerge in the woods that day, smiling, joking around, and even flirting with me subtly. She was so beautiful when she smiled that it hurt me to look at her, but I endured it, because the pleasure quickly outweighed the pain.

I hadn't kissed her all day, waiting to let her make the first move, but she didn't. The last thing I wanted to do was come on too strong again, and scare her away. She was fragile, and despite the comfort that seemed to be settling over her, I knew she needed to do all of this on her own terms - whatever 'this' was.

I tried to keep a tight reign on not just my cock, but also my racing thoughts. If I let them run away too far, I found myself imagining a future with Lacey, and I knew I was kidding myself about that.

The last thing that woman needed was a life in the MC world. She needed to start over and finally have a normal life, filled with all the love and happiness I was sure she would find outside of this secluded forest we lived in.

So, I spent the day with her, focused on teaching her to punch the bag and making her laugh. The sound of her bubbling laughter was like music to my ears, and I couldn't get enough of it. Finally, though, after hours of enjoying her, it got to be too much, and I knew I needed a break if I intended to keep my promise to myself not to rip her clothes off and take her right there beside the creek.

We went back to the clubhouse and she hung out with Grace for awhile before dinner. Afterwards, she retreated to her room and I didn't see her again all evening.

Slade jumped around in front of me, and the Gods began forming a circle around us, chanting and cheering, their bottles in their hands as they got drunker and drunker as the night wore on.

My hand snaked out, making contact with Slade's right cheek, snapping his head around violently. If it weren't for the bloody smile that spread across his face when he looked back at me, I would have thought I had hurt him. But Slade never seemed to get hurt, and if he did, well I'd never seen anyone enjoy pain that much. Except for me. But that was a long, long time ago. These days, I didn't get as much pleasure from it as I used to.

That was the way it goes, I guess.

Getting older changed you, settled you, made you seek out comfort instead of adventure and hell-raising.

I was thinking too much, though. Slade snuck a punch in, and I didn't duck in time, and his fist caught the side of my jaw, whipping my head to the side as the crowd cheered. I stumbled, landing on my ass in the dirt. I looked up as Slade danced around me, the smug grin returning to his ugly face. I shook it off and stood back up, remembering the words of my coach so long ago.

"I can teach you to fight, but I can't teach you how to get up," he told me. And he was right. After killing that guy in the ring, I never learned to get back up myself.

Normally, this is where I would stumble again, and pretend that Slade had gotten the best of me. I loved that goofy dude, and he pouted like a school girl when he lost. But not this time. He was in for a surprise, because I had way too much pent up frustration inside of me tonight, and I had no other outlet except for his self-satisfied mug. Fighting with Slade was the only fighting I really allowed myself to do. I'd never step into the ring again.

I pushed him, provoking him to try to hit me again, which worked. He was so predictable. His right fist shot out, and I ducked under it this time, hooking him just under the chin, sending him flying backwards and landing with a thump on the ground, knocking him dizzy.

I heard a startled gasp behind me, and turned just in time to see Lacey's wide eyes filled with fear and confusion, before she ran away from the group.

"Fuck!" I pushed through the crowd and followed Lacey as she ran into the clubhouse and down the hallway that led to her bedroom. A loud bang rang through the clubhouse as she slammed the door. I stopped short, taking a deep breath and knocking lightly on the door.

The crowd outside had streamed in after us, and I felt the curious gaze of a dozen pairs of eyes drilling into my back.

"Lacey, open up." I whispered. "Please?"

I listened at the door, my mind racing, trying to assess the situation as fast as I could. Why was she so upset? I knocked again.

"Lacey, come on…"

Slowly the door opened, and her face peeked through the crack, streaked with tears.

"Can I come in? Please?"

She nodded, and opened the door, letting me through. I turned to close it behind me, and saw all those eyes still watching.

"Go away, you nosey fucks!" I seethed, before slamming the door.

I turned to see Lacey staring at me. She looked almost afraid, and it killed me to see the tears on her face.

"What's wrong?" I asked.

"What do you mean, what's wrong? You were *fighting*. With Slade. Why would you hurt him like that?"

"What? Lacey, he likes it…I mean, it's just something we do…when we want…oh, fuck, look it doesn't mean anything at all."

"I just don't understand how you could pummel your friend like that…" her voice trailed off and she turned away from me defensively, breaking my heart when I realized she was afraid of me.

"Lacey, listen, babe. Slade and I go way back. He's my best friend. We fight each other all the time. We do it for fun, not because we are trying to hurt each other."

"That makes no sense to me."

"I can see how it wouldn't. People out of the life don't understand. Slade and I use it as an outlet for frustration…it's not real. The other Gods think it's entertaining. It looks a lot worse than it is. I would never hurt him seriously, and he wouldn't hurt me either."

"Well, whatever. I don't know, it just bothers me…" her voice trailed off, and she avoided my eyes.

"Lacey," I said. "Please look at me."

She wouldn't.

"Lacey, why does it bother you?"

Her voice shook as she turned towards me.

"Look, the only violence I've seen was always directed towards me, and it sure as hell wasn't out of love or fun."

"I'm so sorry that happened to you, sweetheart," I said, closing the distance between us, not sure if she would let me close to her, but thanking the heavens that she didn't shrink away when I did.

I reached up to push a strand of hair from her face, and the sight of my bloody knuckles stopped me cold. I smiled at her, shrugging.

"I don't want to get blood on you," I said, pulling away. I sat on her bed and she sat next to me. "I'm sorry I upset you, babe. I had no idea that would happen, but I should have thought it through a little better."

She looked away, silently accusing me of who-knows-what? Of being a monster? She had no idea how right she was, if that was what she was thinking. But not anymore.

"I want to tell you a story. You saw my bag, I told you I was a fighter before, and when you asked why I stopped, I changed the subject." I took a deep breath, the memories flooding back like a burst dam. " I don't like to talk about it...but...well, fuck, there's no other way to say it - I - I killed a guy. In my first fight."

She turned to look at me, but this time, I turned away. I couldn't meet her eyes. Not while I was right there, back in the ring.

"I don't know how it happened, the odds of that shit actually going down on someone's first real fight are astronomical, but it happened. To me"

"What happened afterwards?" she asked quietly.

"Nothing. After that, I couldn't fight anymore."

"That's awful, I'm so sorry, Riot," she said, her voice soft and tender.

"I loved fighting." I continued, the words flowing easier now. "It was in my bones. Once I realized I could do it, it was all I ever thought about. I had bet my whole future on these hands, on my dream." I put my hands out in front of me, looking at them. My weapons. "And I got burned. I did it too well. Or, I did it all wrong. However you want to look at. Either way, I'm a fucking murderer."

Finally, I turned to face her, the tenderness in her eyes a sweet salve on the wound I had just reopened.

"That's why it's safe with me and Slade. He's the only person I fight, unless I have to defend myself, which is rare these days. Most people are smart enough not to fuck with a God. Having this patch, having the brotherhood, that keeps me from having to fight."

"So, I'm sorry I scared you, but I want you to know I would never hurt someone willingly."

"It's okay," she said, a tentative smile lingering on her lips. "I guess I'm just not much of a fighter."

I peered into her eyes and shook my head, once again, completely dumbfounded at the beauty I found there.

"Seems to me, that's exactly what you are. You've been through so much, Lacey. Unthinkable things. Things that most people wouldn't have survived. But you did." I reached up again, cupping her chin and brushing my lips with hers gently, before I continued. "You fought. You won, baby. You won by living through all the shit, you struggled through it, and you did it all on your own, with help from not one single person. You're a warrior, Lacey. Don't you dare forget that."

I kissed her again, stood up and pulled her into my arms.

"You're the most badass fighter I've ever known, Lacey Hope Carrington," I said, looking into those green depths.

She laid her head on my chest, and wrapped her arms around me. Once again, despite my willing it to go away, my cock twitched and hardened in my jeans.

I should be able to control myself more. I was pissed that I couldn't, that my fucking body had more control than I did. I wanted to be a good man for her, not just another asshole in the line of assholes that had treated her badly.

I needed to do the right thing.

And as soon as she turned her stunning eyes up to me again, the tears drying on her cheeks, the desire burned right through me, and I couldn't stop myself.

I caught her lips in mine, and the passion came rushing in, my mouth possessing hers, my tongue parting her lips and darting inside, twirling with hers searchingly, the longing for closeness so strong, so necessary, so intense that I began to press into her until my cock throbbed and rubbed against her wantonly.

She gasped in surprise, and reality came crashing back down, knocking me out of my lusty haze and reminding me that I was doing everything I had vowed not to. Again.

"Shit." I muttered, pulling away from her. "Lacey, I'm so sorry. I'm a shit."

"No, I…" Her lips were red and swollen, and I shook my head, the feelings so fucking overwhelming I was beginning to lose any faith I had in doing the right thing.

I turned away, opened the door, and walked out into the hall, closing the door behind me, leaving her all alone. I swallowed hard, and thundered down the hallway, out the front door past all the gawking Gods, and into the dark sanctuary of the night.

EIGHTEEN

Lacey

The door closed and the tears fell down my cheeks. Riot was hot and cold, and I didn't know what the hell to think. He had kissed me again like he did the first time, and then he just left me alone.

I was so confused, so full of uncertainty, so fucking lost that I couldn't see straight.

You killed Monty, the voice returned.

"Fuck you!" I replied out loud. "Monty fucking deserved it, goddammit!"

Riot's words rang in my head…'you're a fighter'…he had said. Was he right? Or was I just a submissive victim? Why hadn't I managed to kill Monty sooner? Or at least left? The beatings did their job, I guess, because until I had been arrested, until I had that card and Grace's number in my bra, I had never even assigned escaping as an actual possibility.

Something in me had snapped.

I wasn't that woman anymore.

Sure, it had been such an incredibly short time, merely days, and I could still feel the pain of the bruises Monty had left me covered in, I could still see his dead, empty eyes staring at me every time I closed my own, but I was so fucking ready to move on, to start a new life, to get as far away from my past as I possibly could, and as fast as possible, too.

I needed that.

I needed to feel and experience all the things that I had missed. And right now, tonight, that meant Riot. Riot's passion. Riot's lust. Riot's caress. His gentleness and his intense masculine strength all at the same time. I wanted everything he could give me.

And I wanted it right now.

I threw open the door, running down the hallway after him. As I reached the living room, Cherry's eyes locked onto mine, and she nodded encouragingly, pointing to the front door.

"Thank you," I mouthed, running out the front door. I saw the flashlight on the railing, grabbed it and ran to the one place I knew I would find him.

When I reached his spot, his back was to me. He was pummeling the bag, bare-fisted, his shirt thrown on the rock behind him, and a light sheen of sweat covering his tattooed back, shimmering under the moonlight.

I stopped short, watching him from a distance through the trees.

He had called me a warrior, but he was the true warrior. I gazed in awe at his strength as blow after blow landed on the swinging bag.

Warmth and desire washed over me as I watched his savage display of pure masculinity. I wanted those hands on me, pushing and pulling on my flesh, I wanted to feel him inside me, filled up with his passion for me. I ran through the trees, and he stopped punching when he heard me behind him.

"Lacey, I —,"

I held up a hand to stop him.

"No, listen to me, Riot, please?" I pleaded. He stood in front of me, the fire in his eyes a threat to my very sanity as I searched for the right words. "Look, I understand what you're trying to do. Holding back. Wanting to be gentle. And I appreciate it, I really do, so much. But um…" Shyness threatened to overtake me, but I pushed it away. "Look, I need this. You. Me. Whatever this is between us…I need to know what it feels like to say yes. To be wanted, because you want me. Not because you're paying for me. Not because you own me. But because you want me just for me. I want to…*I need to*…know what that feels like. You don't have to be gentle with me, Riot. I can take it, I promise. I - I - I'll love it, I want it, I want you…please, Riot, please show me everything I've missed, please show me what it's really supposed to be like…" I was begging now, but I didn't care.

His eyes darkened with first confusion, then realization, and then the savage passion I had glimpsed earlier. He walked to me, his lips landing on mine in a fury of lust and I met his intensity as much as I could. I was breathless, my knees weakening as he wrapped his arms around me, pulling me close, possessing me and yet somehow, I knew I was still the one in charge.

I had asked for it. And he was going to give it to me.

"Lacey…" his voice was thick with emotion as he tore his lips from mine. "Are you sure?"

"Yes, Riot, please…now, right here, right now…I want to feel you, all of you, please…I just want to forget everything and feel normal for just a little while…please…"

His lips crashed onto mine again and we sank down onto the forest floor, our bed a layer of fallen pine needles. His weight fell on me deliciously, his naked, muscular, tattooed chest pressed hard against mine as I pushed up towards him, and wrapped my legs around his hips.

His kisses grew deeper, stronger, more demanding as he devoured me. Hands trailed over flesh, the need for feeling every inch of him so strong that I felt like I was on fire with it. I wanted to know him. All of him. And I wanted him to know me. Whatever was left of me, I wanted to give it to him.

His hands found the bottom of my t-shirt, tugging it over my head. I reached behind me, unclasping my bra and throwing it to the side.

He gasped and I looked up to meet his gaze. His eyes raged in the moonlight, his hands finding their way to my hardened nipples and heaving breasts. With rough fingers, he traced my moonlit curves, and I melted under his touch.

I pulled him closer with my thighs, his hard cock throbbing against me as I lifted my hips, pressing up into him wantonly, wanting to make it very clear how much I wanted him. He felt huge against me, and I shivered in anticipation as I reached down and pulled at the buttons on his jeans.

One quick pull down over his hips, and his cock sprang forth between us. He groaned as I slipped my hand around him, stroking his massiveness boldly in the dark. His hips bucked, his lips found mine again, and we rocked against each other, moaning through our kisses, the electric heat of the moment fueling our fiery intensity.

Riot pulled his mouth from mine, groaned and began trailing his kisses down my neck and chest, his tongue dipping between my bare breasts, licking and nibbling at my nipples as his hand snaked down and began working at the snap and zipper of my jeans. I unwrapped my thighs reluctantly from his hips, raising up so he could pull them down. I kicked off my shoes, and he pulled them off all the way.

I lay panting in front of him, wearing nothing but my black panties and a few errant leaves and pine needles that had tangled in my hair. He stood up, removing his jeans and boots and throwing them in the pile. He stood naked over me, his burly beauty highlighted by the shadows the moonlit trees threw over his sculpted frame.

He was pure savage masculinity, and with the backdrop of the raw nature surrounding us, he looked right at home, a wild creature of the forest himself.

"Lacey," he grunted, as he kneeled down, hovering over me, the heat in his eyes almost too much to take. "You're the most beautiful thing I've ever seen in my life."

My heart soared. I smiled up at him and wrapped my bare thighs around his naked hips.

"Please, Riot..." I pleaded, all thoughts of anything but him faded from my mind. "Now, baby, please...please..."

He pressed forward, and slipped into me smoothly, his throbbing need filling me completely in one swift thrust. I gasped, my eyes widening as I met his gaze, and I melted into the Earth below, waves of delicious pleasure washing over my body as he began moving his hips, slowly moving in and out of me as he watched my face for any sign of resistance.

He would never find it.

A wildfire of pleasure spread through me, consuming my body with the need for him, for this night, for this moment, for this forest, this new life.

"Yes, oh my god, Riot, yes..." Tears sprang to my eyes, and I let them fall, opening my heart for just this one, safe moment.

Our bodies rocked against each other, melting into one, Riot's heat obliterating anything outside of the two of us, our every movement urgent, desperate. I clung to him, holding on, digging into him with my heels, his hips rising and falling rhythmically as he sank into me over and over.

I whimpered and moaned, every word lost in sensual ecstasy before they could escape from my lips. But words weren't necessary. Riot gave me exactly what I needed from him. He pushed into me, each stroke a lesson in intention - purposeful, strong, precise. The subtle movements of his hands, his hips, his mouth, all skillfully pulling me away from reality and into this magical fantasy of scorching passion.

My hands trailed down to his ass, his muscles flexing under my fingertips with each thrust, each push, each pull away and smooth plunge back into my center.

It had never been like this, this pure rawness mixed with such tender sensuality. I lost myself in Riot's arms, the past melting away from my mind, from my body, leaving nothing but right here, right now, this night under this moon, with this perfect, strong, brutally sexy man.

His breath quickened along with his pace, and soon we were slamming together, over and over, harder and harder, until we reached the edge of consciousness, the heat of our bodies crashing into each other, building the energy and chemistry between us until we exploded into a fiery ball of passion, our souls mingling together above us, and floating away into the moonlit sky, until we lay panting, breathless, spent in each other's arms. The only thing left existing in our world was the pounding rhythm that our beating hearts fell into together.

NINETEEN

Riot

Sunlight burned through my window, the heat searing my back as I sank my swollen cock back into Lacey's deliciously sensual center.

We hadn't slept. I couldn't get enough of her, and the dance of wonder and delight playing across her face with every stroke, every lick, every kiss was intoxicating and addicting.

She moaned, purred, bucked and clawed at me as I unleashed my passion on every inch of her. She tasted like fresh, sweet cherries, and I spent hours tasting her, starting so slow she was whimpering, drawing her pleasure out of her with purposeful strokes of my tongue and nibbling and sucking and licking until she was writhing on the bed below me, a beautiful masterpiece of feminine bliss.

I had never felt more like a man in my life. The years of boxing, being a God, riding, fighting with Slade - none of that had compared to the deep, savage masculinity that coursed through my veins as I watched her come to life under my fingertips.

By the time the birds had started chirping, I was afraid I would hurt her if we didn't stop soon. But she was so willing, so wet, so blissed-out, that no matter how many times she came, she wanted more and more.

Luckily, my cock was happily up to the task.

Our bodies fit together perfectly, her soft pussy wrapped around me, along with her sexy legs, and we rocked together in the sunlight, our kisses soft, wet, gentle.

I felt like we had been kissing each other all our lives.

Thoughts of the future kept creeping in the back of my mind, and instead of letting them take over, I kept making love to her, afraid to stop, afraid to let her go, afraid that if we stopped we would never get back to this heavenly place we had discovered together.

Shuddering, our bodies once again crashed into an explosion of heat as we came together. We were drenched in sweat, our bodies sliding together sensuously as I kissed her deeply, as she moaned and cooed.

Gently, I slid out of her, laying down beside her and pulling her to me. She laid her head on my chest, and closed her eyes and we drifted off to sleep for the first time.

TWENTY

Lacey

I woke up to the hot afternoon sun scorching my bare skin. Riot's bed was right next to the window, and despite all the trees surrounding the clubhouse, his room was in the one unprotected spot. The heat was brutal, and I raised my head to look around.

Riot was nowhere to be seen.

I sighed, stretched and smiled the biggest smile I had ever smiled in my life. He was amazing. The things he had done to my body were amazing. I had never felt so alive.

I was free.

I was happy.

I jumped up, dressed, and ran back down the hall to my room. I had to pass the living room, but luckily, it was empty. I didn't want to explain to anyone why I was coming out of Riot's room.

I jumped in the shower as soon as I reached my room, my smile still plastered across my face. My body was still singing from the intense pleasure I had felt with Riot. I knew I was missing out on a lot, but I had no idea I was missing out on *that!*

HONEY PALOMINO

I washed my hair, and a huge wave of gratitude washed over me. Riot was the most perceptive, intuitive lover, and he concentrated on making me shake, shudder and come all night and all morning.

My lips, breasts and every inch of my flesh was still on fire with his touch. He had been gentle at the right times, and not so gentle exactly when I needed it.

I didn't know all the things that I read about in books had the potential of really happening. I thought happiness was a fairy tale, and the elusive man that actually cared about your pleasure was an illusion. Riot was quickly showing me something that was a complete contrast to any other experiences I had had.

Not one of Monty's friends had ever been interested in anything I was feeling. Usually, it was a quick session of them grunting over me for five minutes. The other times, it was just a lot of acting out some stupid fantasy they had.

I had never come like that before. Not like last night. Riot had brought me over the edge over and over again, until I was a babbling mess of shuddering flesh. Sure, I had masturbated, but even I didn't know how to do some of the things Riot had done to me.

I was smitten.

And what did that mean?

Now that I was out of Riot's arms, reality began crashing down around me. I was supposed to be leaving. Starting over. Assuming a new identity.

But, suddenly, the last thing I wanted to do was leave this ramshackle paradise in the woods with my new lover.

You killed Monty, the familiar whisper of my conscience curled up in my ear, but this time, again, nothing happened. My heart didn't speed up, I felt not one pang of guilt, fear or trepidation.

I felt nothing but happiness.

I've always heard that everything happens for a reason, but I could never really believe it. How could all the shit my mom did to me have

101

any good reason? Or Monty? There was never any nugget of reason to any of that, as far as I could see. I was just doing what I needed to do to survive, and never thought I'd really ever get out of it.

But if all of that wouldn't have happened, I would never be standing here today. It was crazy to think about, really. If my mom hadn't been such a monster. If Monty hadn't bought me, hadn't decided to use me to gain more money and power by selling me to his friends, if he hadn't sent me on that last date with the weird egg guy. If I hadn't been walking down that street, if I hadn't been stopped by the cop, if I hadn't gotten in the car with him. If I hadn't been in jail, I never would have met the woman who gave me Grace's card.

And if I hadn't killed Monty, I never would have called.

And if I never called, then I never would have met Riot, and last night would have never happened.

I sighed, and realized…I was starting to finally heal.

Escaping from Monty, reaching out to Solid Ground, opening my heart to Riot, those things were finally allowing my soul to heal, if only little bits at a time.

And all because a woman slipped me a business card.

A business card.

Oh, shit!

Where's the fucking card?

Suddenly, I realized I hadn't seen it since I had arrived here. Grace had explicitly instructed me on the phone to destroy the card, but I had shoved it in my bag, wanting for some reason to hold on to it, just in case. In case what? I don't know. In case I needed it again.

I flew out of the bathroom, naked, still wet from the shower, and began riffling through my unpacked bag. I looked in all the pockets, and the pockets of all my jeans, to no avail. I searched around the room, my heart beating wildly by now, the frantic feeling of having royally fucked up washing over me and driving that blissed-out peacefulness away faster than it had arrived.

I couldn't find it anywhere.

I stood in the middle of the room, tears streaming down my face, as I realized how badly I had fucked up. How could I have left that behind?

I dressed quickly and ran out the door of the clubhouse. It was strange that the clubhouse was still completely empty, but I didn't think about it too much at that point. But when I reached Grace and Ryder's cabin, and they didn't answer my persistent knocking, I walked back to the clubhouse slowly, trying to think of what to do.

When I returned, I realized I was all alone, which only fueled the insipid paranoia that quickly crept up my spine and settled in the back of my skull like a dull ache.

What had I fucking done?

TWENTY-ONE

Grace

"Howdy, Ms. Grace," John, the bartender, said, as I walked through the swinging door of the Rodeo Roadhouse. It was the closest, and only, place to get a decent burger near the clubhouse, and I needed a break from the cabin.

"Hi, John!"

"Where's Ryder today?"

"He had some business to attend to with the club today in Portland. Just me today."

I nodded to Susie, his waitress, when she walked out of the kitchen. Susie and John had become familiar faces after Ryder had brought me here the first time. I had been trying so hard to remember something, anything, about where I had come from, who I was, and Ryder had brought me here for our first public outing after I woke up from my very long slumber.

The things I had finally remembered still haunted me, and I'd be lying if I said I was completely glad I remembered. Sometimes there are things in the past you just wish you could wash away. But it doesn't work that way, does it?

That's why I was here, needing a break from the work I had chosen to do. It was brutal, knowing that every second of every day there was some woman out in the world being abused. Someone that needed saving, because for whatever reason, they couldn't save themselves.

Like Lacey. Lacey's story wove through my head as I waited for my order. I shuddered thinking about the hell she had been put through, not only at Monty's hands, but at her mother's. I had a suspicion the horrors her mother put her through had left even deeper scars than the men who had used her body for their own perverted pleasure.

I knew first hand the devastation that a wicked mother could cause, the kind that lingered deep under your skin, changing you in ways you'd never imagine, making you do things you'd never normally do, if you been blessed with a loving, caring, nurturing mother. It broke you right open when you didn't have that basic need met.

And I could see it had done that to Lacey. She was hard on the outside, but I could see through the cracks. She was a mess inside, lost, confused.

Which made me half happy and half concerned that she had connected so strongly with Riot. Riot was a good man, but was he really what Lacey needed right now?

I wasn't sure about that. She was the opposite of me. I had been independent all my life, and meeting Ryder had changed all of that. I couldn't imagine my life now without him.

But Lacey had depended on that sick fuck, Monty, so heavily, that I really felt she needed to see what it was like to be on her own.

Ryder and the Gods had gone to Portland this morning for club business, and Riot had been given the task of riding to Salem to obtain Lacey's fake id, birth certificate, and social security card. I had a friend in the Capital from my days as a cop. Sarah was easily able to obtain things like that, and I was so grateful for her. She had proven to be a good friend, and one of the few that I trusted.

When I went to let Lacey know where I was going, and that she would be alone for an hour or so, she was sleeping peacefully in Riot's bed. I didn't disturb her, left her a note in the kitchen, and took off.

She looked happy for the first time.

Everything was falling into place nicely. As soon as she had arrived at the clubhouse, I made a series of phone calls that put the ball in motion, not only to get her a new ID, but also a new apartment and a job, too. I was confident we would be able to get her safely set up somewhere else, where Monty's people and the cops looking for her wouldn't find her.

Even with my connections on the force, I didn't trust the police in this situation. If she hadn't killed the fucking Mayor of Seattle, then maybe I could ask them to quietly close the case and look the other way while I got Lacey placed. But not now. There was no one I knew on the force that could help with this situation.

Susie brought me my burger and I thanked her. She lingered at my table.

"A woman came by yesterday," she said. "Asking questions. Reporter, she claimed. Said she was following up on a lead. Asked about the club. Said she was looking for a girl from Seattle."

Shit. My heart began pounding in my chest.

"Oh, yeah? You get any more info?"

"She gave me her card," Susie replied, pulling a card out of the pocket of her apron. "Cute little blonde with a perky nose and perkier tits. Told me to call her if I heard anything."

I looked at the card.

Diana Trudeau
Investigative Reporter
KATU News
Portland, Oregon

The woman from the news the other day. Just fucking lovely.

"You answer any of her questions?" I asked Susie.

"Nope," she replied with a wink, as she refilled my water glass. "I don't talk to strangers."

I nodded, and smiled gratefully as she walked away.

My suspicions confirmed, I downed my lunch as fast as I could and went out to my car. I sat behind the wheel, my head spinning with anxiety, when I heard the distinctive ring of the safe phone.

I dug it out of my purse, looked at the caller ID, and answered quickly.

"What's the password?" I asked.

"Who is this?" A gruff male voice barked.

"What's the password?" I asked again.

The resounding click in my ear told me everything I needed to know.

TWENTY-TWO

Riot

I was walking on air. I hadn't been this happy since…well, fuck, since never. I tried all day to wipe the shit-eating grin off my face, but try as I might, I failed.

Lacey's skin was still sliding under my fingertips, her soft moans echoing in my ears, her incredible body writhing and undulating against mine, those tight thighs still wrapped around me. I couldn't shake the feeling of still being in bed with her. My mind didn't want to let go, as much as my body didn't hours ago, as I left her peacefully sleeping in my bed.

By the time I made it to Salem, I was finally beginning to resemble some form of the man I used to be. I was Riot, goddammit. Letting my mind be clouded like that left me vulnerable, and I couldn't afford to be vulnerable.

I needed to make sure I wasn't being watched, or followed. I needed to retrieve the package from Sarah, and be on my way back to the clubhouse safely. All of that was fairly easy to do, as long as I kept my wits about me. As long as I didn't get carried away by thoughts of

Lacey's gorgeous body laid out before me, waiting, willing, begging for more of me…

See? I did it again.

Stop it! I commanded myself as my bike roared up to the park I was meeting Sarah at. *Lacey's life depends on this!*

I managed to wipe the smile from my face as I parked, took off my helmet, and looked around. A few dozen people were milling around, some jogging, some walking their dogs, and others just laying on blankets. A typical day. Nothing to worry about.

I spotted Sarah sitting on a bench by the pond, feeding the ducks that had gathered around her. I walked over, feeling the familiar stares that my cut always seemed to invite. I ignored them, and sat down with Sarah.

"Hey there," she said. Sarah was a portly, friendly woman that I had tremendous respect for. She took great risks to help out Solid Ground, and I suspected she had a reason of her own to want to help. If there was one thing I had learned these last few months, it was that other survivors would do anything to help someone else out of the same situation they endured.

She handed me a thick, unmarked envelope. I tucked it inside the pocket of my cut, and thanked her. She smiled serenely, turning her attention back to the ducks as I walked back to my bike, making sure to take in the faces of everyone around me, just in case.

The ride back home was long, but very nice. Riding had become my life, and I enjoyed it tremendously. My time on my bike was therapeutic. My thoughts cleared, the cloud of being drunk on Lacey had dissipated just slightly, and I roared back to the clubhouse with a sense of focus and fortitude. My cock, unfortunately, was just as laser locked on wanting more of Lacey, so I drove back with the biggest, most uncomfortable hard on I'd ever had in my life.

An hour and a half later, I was almost back to the turn off for the clubhouse when I noticed a shiny, black sedan behind me. I passed the turn off to the clubhouse and headed towards the coast, making a turn off the 6 and then North onto the 101. The car turned with me, and after making a few more turns, I was now convinced they were following me.

I had to lose them before I could go back home. And my cock really, really wanted to go home.

I pulled into a gas station and went inside, watching the black sedan circle around the block twice before I went back out. As soon as they were out of sight, I went South, back down the 101. Quickly turning off onto a side street that led to the beach, I hid my bike behind a truck, and watched. As soon as the car circled back, and its occupants saw my bike gone, they turned around and headed right past me, not seeing me or my bike. Their windows were darkly tinted, and I couldn't see inside, but it was obvious that was no cop car.

I waited ten minutes, then drove back to the clubhouse, keeping an eye out for the sedan, before I turned onto the unmarked road that led to the clubhouse.

When I got there, Grace and Ryder were on the porch, their heads close together as they talked animatedly.

"What's up?" I asked, as I parked my bike.

"Susie at the Roadhouse said some reporter had been sniffing around. Asked about the club. Said they were looking for a girl from Seattle." Grace pushed a card at me, and I nodded.

"The reporter from the news we saw the other day," I said. "The one with the perky tits."

"Yeah, and apparently a good nose!" Ryder replied. "How'd she find us?"

"Good question. I think Monty's people are on our trail, too. I went to Salem, and when I got back, I realized I was being followed. Some goons in a black van. They were easy to lose."

"Fuck!" Ryder said, exasperation growing on his face.

"We'll figure it out," Grace said reassuringly. "But there's one more thing. I got a call. On the safe phone. It was a man, and they didn't know the safe word. They hung pretty quickly. Think you can trace the number?"

"Yeah, definitely," I said, taking the phone from her.

"You tell Lacey?" I asked.

"No, we just got here."

"Tell Lacey what?" Lacey opened the screen door of the clubhouse and walked out onto the porch with us.

TWENTY-THREE

Lacey

"It's all my fault," I confessed.

I fucked up big time. And I knew it as soon as I saw the look on their faces as I walked out onto the porch.

"No, it's not," Riot said, pulling me into his arms. They had just explained about the phone call, the reporter, and the people following Riot.

"It is. I'm so sorry, you guys, but I have to tell you something."

They all looked at me, waiting. My stomach sank as I let the words flow from my mouth. They had tried to save me, and I had screwed it all up.

"The card. I left your card at my apartment. I just realized it this morning, and I looked all through my stuff, but I can't find it anywhere, I'm so fucking sorry."

They groaned in unison.

"Fuck…okay, well it still doesn't make sense. Now we know how the caller got the number, but I certainly didn't give him any information so how does the reporter and Monty's people know to look here?" Grace said.

"Unless someone at the crime scene leaked it, which is entirely possible. Monty had friends in the highest and lowest of places," Ryder replied.

"Okay. So, however it happened, we need to move you. If anyone comes sniffing around, it's important that you aren't here."

"Oh," I replied, my head dropping to Riot chest. He was still holding me, and the last thing I wanted to do was go somewhere else.

"You can't go to your new place yet. All the details aren't finalized yet, and we need to make sure you aren't followed," Grace said.

"She can go to Eugene," Riot suggested.

"Who's Eugene?" I asked.

"Not who, where. We have a branch of Gods in Eugene, you can go stay at their clubhouse. We can trust them. Right, Ryder?"

"Yeah, she'll certainly be safe there. That means we have to let the Eugene Gods know what we've been up to. I'm not certain I want to expand our circle. It's important that we keep Solid Ground underground."

"Do we have to tell them the truth?" I asked.

Ryder paused before answering.

"Maybe not the whole truth. I'll give them a call." Ryder stood up and walked into the clubhouse, pulling his phone out of his pocket.

"I'm so sorry, Grace," I said. "I feel awful. I thought for sure I had the card, but I must have missed it somehow when I was packing."

"That's okay, babe. That's why we have the safe word system in place. You didn't tell anyone the safe word, did you?"

"No! No way."

"Everything is going to be okay, don't worry, Lacey. You'll be fine at the Eugene clubhouse. They're a...interesting...group," Riot said.

"Um..." The thought of being with a whole new group of strangers made me want to scream. "Can you come with me?" I asked Riot, staring up at him.

"You bet, babe."

He leaned down and kissed me gently. I felt Grace's eyes on us, and heard her sigh as she walked back into the clubhouse after Ryder.

TWENTY-FOUR

Riot

"You should pack a few things," I said in between laying kisses on Lacey.

"Thank you for coming with me," she said, her big eyes turned up to me.

"I couldn't let you go alone. Sorry for leaving you alone this morning, by the way." I remembered the package in my vest, and pulled it out and handed it to her.

"What's this?" she asked.

"Your new ID. Social Security card, and birth certificate, too."

She began to open it, but I stopped her.

"That's for your eyes only, babe. For security. It's one of the rules of Solid Ground. Only you know your new identity."

"Oh," she said sadly.

"What's wrong?" I asked, peering into her eyes, trying to ignore the urge to shuffle her off to my room and pick up where we left off this morning.

"I don't know," she replied, shaking her head. "I'll go pack, I guess."

"Okay, babe, we'll ride out in a few hours," I replied, as she walked sullenly back into the clubhouse. I followed her in, and Grace and Ryder confronted me as soon as Lacey was out of sight.

"Couldn't keep it in your pants, huh, Romeo?" Ryder asked.

"Not a good idea, Riot!" Grace said.

"What?" Fuck, this was the last thing I needed. Grief from these two. "It's nothing."

"Oh, yeah? Well, then that's even worse," Grace said, her voice rising in anger.

"No! That's not what I meant," I protested. "Look, it's not what you think. I'm not just using her or something. Fuck, give me a break!"

"Look, Lacey needs to be thinking about her future, and starting a whole new life. She doesn't need to get mixed up in your life."

"My life?" I exclaimed. "I don't really have much of one, if you hadn't noticed."

"Look, man, just keep it together. She'll be starting a new life soon. Your job is to protect her until she gets there."

"Yeah, I got it," I replied gruffly.

"You got your piece?" Ryder asked, as he slid a box of bullets across the kitchen table at me.

"Yeah," I replied, the weight of the gun tucked in my waistband a constant reminder that I was never without my backup protection. My fists were always my first line of defense. I grabbed the bullets, and walked back outside.

I didn't want to hear their shit, as much as I knew what they were saying was true. Every step Lacey and I made was designed to get her farther and farther away from me, and now that I had a taste of her, I just wanted to bring her as close to me as possible.

How was I ever going to let her go now that I found her? Nobody had ever made me feel like that in bed before. Hell, nobody had ever made me feel anything in bed at all. There was something real, something basic, some intuitive need between Lacey and I that

116

demanded to be acknowledged. And as much as I wanted to resist it, I couldn't help but embrace it.

The fact that she wasn't mine? That the last thing she needed was a man, *this man*, in her life? Those facts just kept getting pushed to the back of my mind, until the moment came when I had to say goodbye, when I could deny them no longer.

Grace and Ryder left moments later.

"Lacey's resting. How about you let her get some sleep, Casanova?" Grace said, smiling as she and Ryder walked hand in hand back to their cabin.

Hours passed as I waited on the porch for the sun to go down. It seemed like forever, and the moments inched by, an excruciating reminder that I was that much closer to that final goodbye I knew I would have to eventually say to Lacey.

As if to remind me that that time wasn't here just yet, Lacey walked out of the clubhouse, the fading sunlight shining through her flimsy white shirt as the light breeze made it dance around her body. She was stunning.

I swallowed hard, images of her moaning, writhing body dancing uncontrollably through my head, tempting me to turn her around and lead her back to bed.

But, I didn't.

No, I went against every instinct I had. I didn't touch her, I didn't kiss her, I didn't make love to her like a starving man. I handed her a leather jacket and a helmet.

"You ready?"

"Yep," she replied, putting her backpack down and placing the helmet over her black curls.

"Can you um…help me?" Lacey asked, turning to me, the straps of her helmet outstretched.

"Sure." I lifted her chin, and fitted the clasps together, adjusting the length of the strap until it was tightly holding the helmet to her head. I looked into her eyes, turning away when I saw the questions in her eyes.

I had all the same questions, and not one fucking answer for her.

"Everything's going to be okay, darlin', don't worry," I whispered.

She half-grinned, and we mounted the bike. We rode off down the dirt road, the clubhouse fading from view behind us.

We were about an hour down the road, just getting into Portland, when Lacey tapped me on the back. I turned my head and she yelled at me.

"Gotta pee!" she yelled. I nodded to her and she wrapped her hands and thighs around me again, tightening her grip on my body as we thundered through the tunnel that led into the southwest part of the city.

I stopped at the first diner I found.

"Thank you!" Lacey said, as she took off her helmet.

"You hungry?" I asked. She nodded and ran into the diner quickly. I laughed.

"I'll get us a table," I said to her back. I took a minute to walk around the parking lot, stretching my legs and hands. Riding for a long time took a toll on your body, and the older I got, the more it hurt.

The diner shared a parking lot with a motel, and it was filled with empty cars. The streets were streaming with occupied ones. I hated coming into the city these days. I had once loved it, loved the electric vibrance of it all, but not anymore. Now, I preferred staying at the clubhouse as much as I could. Being alone was comfortable for me. And those secluded woods provided me with a sense of peace that I craved, even if it was within the chaotic setting of the clubhouse.

Aches, pains, and the need for serenity. I was starting to sound like a very old man.

I walked in to the diner and the hostess led me to a table in the back. When Lacey found me, I was looking out the window, a million miles away.

"Feel better?" I asked.

"Yes, tons. Sorry, I should have gone before I left."

"That's okay. Gives us a chance to grab a bite before we get there. The Eugene Gods don't have any women like Grace or Cherry to keep the fridge stocked."

"Oh," she replied, her face falling again.

"You don't want to go," I said.

"Well…I mean, don't get me wrong, it's not that I'm not grateful. And I know I screwed this whole thing up and that's why I have to leave. I know it's all my fault. But I - I - I…well, I was just getting comfortable at your clubhouse," she added, shyly.

I laughed out loud, much louder than I intended to.

"You definitely looked comfortable this morning when I left you sleeping in my bed," I replied.

"Yes," she said, her eyes shifting down. "I did."

"Hey."

"Hey," I repeated, when she wouldn't meet my eyes. She raised them finally, and I smiled at her. "It's all going to be okay, babe, I promise."

I was lying through my teeth. What the hell did I know?

"I hope you're right," she replied, her voice shaking. She had tears in her eyes, and I was reminded once again how frightened she must be.

"The Eugene Gods are just fine, don't worry. And I won't leave you alone for a minute. You're safe with me."

"Thank you, Riot. But what about afterwards?"

"After what?"

"After I leave, to start my new life…" Her eyes fell to the table, and all the questions I saw there earlier came back.

I sighed.

"I don't know, babe. But what I do know is that Grace is great at her job. She wouldn't be sending you anywhere that wasn't safe."

"That's not what I meant," she replied, quietly.

"What then?"

"I meant…well, us…oh, nevermind."

"Us?" I asked.

"Look, I get it, there's no 'us'. I shouldn't have said that." Tears fell down her cheeks.

"Oh, hey, don't do that…" I dabbed at her cheeks with a napkin, and grabbed her hand.

"I'm sorry," she said.

"You have nothing to apologize for. I don't know what's going to happen. I've been thinking about it a lot, though. We'll figure something out. Maybe Grace will let us bend the rules a little, and we can stay in contact."

I knew that wasn't likely, but what was I going to tell her?

She perked up a little, though, and we ate slowly, taking our time before we had to get back on the road. Before we knew it, it was after ten and the diner was closing.

Hand in hand, we walked back to the bike.

I saw the puddle next to my bike right away. My heart pounded as I scanned the parking lot and pulled the gun from my waistband, all at the same time that I pushed Lacey behind me.

"Get back!" I commanded.

"What's wrong?" she asked.

"Someone fucked with my bike," I said, as I pointed to the puddle at my feet. There was not a soul in sight, and the few parked cars in the lot were empty. I put my gun away, and leaned down, poking a finger in the puddle, and smelling it.

"Brake fluid. Fuck! They cut my lines."

"Who would do that?" she asked, her voice shaking in fear.

"Someone who didn't want us to leave."

"What do we do now?" she asked.

"Well, that's a good question." I wouldn't be able to get replacement parts until tomorrow. I could call the Gods to come get us, but the last thing we needed to do was return to the clubhouse. I eyed the motel, and once again, my head was filled with images of Lacey splayed out in front of me, her warm, inviting body just begging me to devour it.

"Let's get a room."

TWENTY-FIVE

Lacey

I woke up the next morning starving.

After talking to Ryder on the phone, we had decided to stay put for the night, but not after much convincing on Riot's part. Ryder wanted to come get us, but Riot convinced him to let us stay and get the bike fixed this morning.

We spent the entire night making love. I was beginning to think he had sold his soul to the devil for that amazingly skillful mouth. I had never come so hard in my life, and with every kiss, every lick, every stroke of his tongue, he took me to places I had never even imagined existed.

My body melted under his assault, submitting to him completely, letting him show me everything I had been missing in that tiny hotel room. He insisted all night that I tell him everything I liked, and didn't like.

They almost didn't let us get a room, and I was convinced my loud moaning would get us kicked out. Neither one of us had a credit card. But apparently, my pleading and Riot's flexing, convinced the clerk to show us a little mercy.

By the time the sun woke me up, Riot was passed out next to me, his face scrunched up on the pillow next to me, drooling. It was so fucking adorable, there was no way in hell I was going to disturb him.

I delicately removed myself from the bed, making sure not to wake him. I dressed quietly, grabbed the hotel key, a twenty from Riot's wallet on the dresser, and walked out into the blazing sunshine, after scribbling a note for him to let him know where I was going.

The diner was dead at this early hour, and I sat at the breakfast counter while I waited for our order. My body was on fire, my flesh deliciously swollen, the soreness a constant reminder of Riot's touch.

It was obvious that the feelings I had for Riot were mutual. Monty's men had never been like that with me. Riot gripped onto me like he never intended to let go. He kissed me and fucked me like my pleasure was the only thing in the world that mattered to him.

And holy fuck did he know to please me. It was like someone gave him a blueprint to my body, and then handed him the only key.

By the time he was done with me, my skin was singing, begging for more of his sweet melody.

My stomach growled, teaching me something new this morning - voracious sex made one very hungry! I had never experienced this before, but apparently, it was very true. And if I was this hungry, then I knew Riot, who had done almost all of the 'work' last night, must be famished.

My order came up, and I paid for it and walked back out into the sunshine. Since it was early, there were only a few cars parked. I was crossing the lot, heading back to the motel, bags of hot food in my hand, when I heard a car door open behind me.

I turned to see two very large men emerge from the car, and begin walking towards me. I picked up my pace, and pulled the hotel key from the pocket of my jeans. Stupidly, I had left my cell phone in the room. The men continued to follow me, and I started running. They began chasing me, and I dropped the food, breaking into a sprint across the lot as the skin on the back of my neck stood up.

I was almost to the door that led into our room, and I began panting, running as fast as I could now to escape them. My foot caught on the curb as I tried to jump up to the sidewalk, and I landed right on my face. Quickly, I jumped back up to my feet, but it was too late.

They towered over me, and I looked up straight into the barrel of a gun.

I took a deep breath, and yelled as loud as I possibly could.

"RIOT!"

TWENTY-SIX

Riot

I heard Lacey's cry before my eyes opened. I bolted out of bed, naked and panicked, looking around the room.

She wasn't here.

I barreled through the door of the motel, just in time to see a black sedan peeling out of the parking lot, Lacey struggling in the backseat, and her screams echoing in my ears.

I hopped on my bike, for a split second forgetting that I was naked, my bike was broken, and that I didn't even have the fucking keys, but reality quickly came crashing down on me.

"Lacey!" I jumped off, screaming, running after the car. It was no use. By the time I got around the corner, it was gone.

"Motherfucker!" I yelled, my fists pumping the air. Never in my life have I wanted to hit something so badly.

What the fuck just happened?

What the fuck was I going to do now?!

I looked around the parking lot frantically, searching for some solution. Unless I stole a car, I had no other options.

I had to call Ryder.

I began running back to my room, when I heard a soft voice call to me.

"Hey, you're Riot, right?" I turned to see the perky blonde reporter from the news the other day. She stood by the ice machine, quietly staring at me, alone and a complete contrast to my panicked state.

"You're that fucking reporter!" I sneered.

She walked up to me slowly, her eyes glued to my naked body.

"I'm Diana Trudeau, KATU News," she closed the distance between us, and held out her card. I stared it blankly.

"I don't have time for your shit," I said, turning to go back to my room.

"Sir, please? If I could have just a minute of your time?"

"Fuck off!" I growled, my blood boiling in my veins.

"I can help you!"

"How do you know my name?" I snarled.

"I - I've been following you! Well, sort of. I know your name, because I just heard that woman yell it before they put her in the car. And I saw you together last night. In the diner."

I turned to look at her, and thundered back to her.

"What are you fucking talking about? Are you the one that cut my fucking brake line?"

"No! Like I said, I - I - I've been following you. Well, Lacey Carrington, really. But since she's with you...well, anyway. But those men that just took her?"

"What about them?" I asked.

"I know where they're staying. I think they're Monty Patterson's men, but I'm not sure. They're definitely not cops. Dressed way too nice for that, you know?" she shrugged. "They've been following you, too. So, I guess I've been following all of you."

"You got a fucking car?" I asked, my mind racing.

"Yes!" she said, her voice shaking.

"Stay here!" I said, yelling over my shoulder as I walked away. "I have to get dressed. Don't fucking go anywhere, you hear me?"

"Darlin'," she replied, her eyes focused squarely on my junk, "with a package like that I - well, I'm not going anywhere."

TWENTY-SEVEN

Lacey

They put something dark over my head as soon as the door slammed shut behind us. I screamed, wiggled, tried to push them off of me. But they were so fucking strong. One of them pressed his hand hard against my mouth, digging my tooth painfully into my lip. I tasted blood, and struggled harder.

"We've got a fucking tiger on our hands here," the man holding me grunted as he struggled to contain me.

"Just hold on to her. We aren't going far," a deep voice boomed from the front seat.

I turned and kicked, my legs flailing wildly and aimlessly, looking for flesh to make contact with. A resounding crack followed immediately by an angry grunt.

"You bitch! That fucking hurt!" His hands gripped my arms tighter and he pushed me roughly against the seat. He shifted beside me and I felt the cold, hard steel push against my temple.

"Try it again, bitch," he snarled in my ear. I swallowed, and stopped moving.

"Don't fucking shoot her, goddammit!" His companion warned.

"If she fucking kicks me one more time, I'm gonna off the little bitch. I don't give one fuck. You know how I hate to be kicked!"

"Alright, alright, shut the fuck up. We need her alive. We're almost there."

"I'm not kidding, bitch," the man beside me pressed the gun harder into my flesh to make his point. "Not a fucking muscle."

I struggled to regain my breath, my adrenaline shooting through my brain, the panic threatening to overwhelm me. I had to stay still. I had to find a fucking way out of this.

What kind of stupid idiot was I? I had to leave the room without Riot. I had to go get fucking breakfast! *Breakfast!*

Now, I was fucked. Riot's bike didn't work, thanks to these two, probably, and there was no way he would ever find me. I didn't even know if he heard me scream. He was sound asleep when I left.

I was completely at their fucking mercy.

All I had was myself, and that wasn't much.

You killed Monty, the voice sounded in my head.

Well, yeah, there was that. Which is no doubt why these guys want to kill me. Or did they? He had said they wanted me alive. Why? What good was I to anyone alive? Especially Monty's people.

Maybe I could get out of this somehow. Maybe Riot had heard me, but I doubted it.

Maybe a fucking miracle will happen, I thought sarcastically. *Because miracles so frequently happened to Lacey Hope Carrington.*

Fuck!

I cursed myself once again for leaving the room. I had been so ridiculously blissed out from spending the night with Riot that I simply had not thought it through. I should have known I was in danger.

I did know! I just…forgot for a minute. I don't know. Of course people were looking for me. I had murdered a goddamned Mayor, for fuck's sake. And I knew the names of all his fucked up, perverted friends, several of whom would be very upset if I revealed those names to anyone.

It didn't matter that I had changed my appearance, had left town. I knew they would stop at nothing to find me. I didn't know I was going to be the one that made it so impossibly easy for them.

Riot is going to be so pissed off at me...

"Here we go," the driver said, as the car slowed and turned right.

"Get down!" The man holding me pushed me down to the floorboard roughly.

"I'm going to pull up to the door, I'll let you know when the coast is clear." The front door opened. Slammed shut. Footsteps.

Seemed like we waited forever, the seconds ticking by with only the sound of my panting in stereo in the sack over my head.

The man shifted in the seat, then pulled the cloth from my head. I looked up at him, his beady crow like eyes staring back at me angrily.

"I'm not going to forget that kick, bitch," he snarled. "Now, we're going to get out slowly. No funny business, or I swear to you I will rip your fucking brains out of your pretty little head, and then go back for that pretty boyfriend of yours, you got me?"

I nodded, silently, my blood pumping so hard through my veins I was sure they would burst.

"Good. Let's go," he said, opening the door, and pulling me out of the car. I winced as the sun hit my eyes. Swiftly, he ushered me past the car, and up to a door. Quickly, I turned my head and saw we were at a motel off a fairly busy road. I scanned the road, and saw no sign of Riot.

*Of course not. You're fucked, remember? You killed Monty. Time to pay the price now...*the voice had learned a few new words.

The man shoved me over the threshold and I stumbled to the floor as he slammed the door behind me.

I smelled her before I saw her.

Chanel number five.

My eyes adjusted and I saw the black velvet stilettos right in front of my face. Slowly, my eyes trailed up black-stockinged legs, the leopard print dress a vivid reminder of my past.

She always loved leopard print.

By the time I reached her face, I was almost curious. Years had passed, and time was, as predicted, not kind to her.

"Hey, baby," she whispered, a sick, blood-red smile spreading across her weathered face, tightening the corners of her evil, dead eyes.

"Hey, Mom."

TWENTY-EIGHT

Riot

I threw all our shit into the reporter's car, and we hauled ass down the street. I called Ryder on the way.

I took a few deep breaths as the phone rang, trying to figure out what to say. Hell, trying to figure out what the fuck had just happened.

How could Lacey be gone? How the fuck could I have let that happen? I had fallen asleep on the job, naively thinking she was safe if we were in bed together. How the fuck did she get outside?

I knew that was going to be the first thing Ryder asked me, and I didn't have an answer.

I was right.

I had barely gotten the words out that Lacey was taken and he asked exactly that.

"What the fuck? Why did you let her out of your sight, Riot?"

"I don't know, man. We - we - I was asleep. I don't know, she must have gotten up before me or something. Pancakes, I think...I - fuck I don't fucking know!"

"Pancakes? What the fuck are you talking about, goddammit?"

Ryder growled at me through the phone, and it took all my strength not to growl back. There was nobody on this fucking Earth more angry than me right now, not even Ryder.

"Look, I think she went for breakfast," I said, taking a deep breath, trying to explain myself better. "I heard a scream, I woke up, and she wasn't there. When I ran outside, she had been shoved in the back of a car and driven away. I saw some fucking pancakes on the ground, I don't know. Look, there's more - that reporter, from the news the other day?"

"Reporter? What the fuck, Riot?"

"I know - look, she was there - she saw everything, she said she had been following us. She knows where the guys who took Lacey are staying."

"What the fuck?" Ryder asked.

"I know, dude, listen, I'm in the car with her right now. She's taking me to their hotel."

I looked over at her, trying to remember her name.

"What's your fucking name?" I asked.

"I - I - gave you my card," she replied. She looked terrified, her hands shaking on the wheel.

I glared at her.

"Diana. D-Diana T-T-Trudeau…" she said, finally.

"Her name is Diana Trudeau," I continued, turning my attention back to Ryder. "She's taking me there now. Where are we going?" I asked her.

"Oh…um…the Travelodge on Barbur Boulevard."

"Brother, we're headed to the Travelodge on Barbur Boulevard. I can fix this. I'll get Lacey, I'll save —,"

"— you'll do no such thing, goddammit, Riot!" Ryder interrupted. "You fucking stay right there until the Gods get there. We'll be there in an hour. You just fucking wait, you understand me? You don't know what you're walking into."

"Ryder, look, I understand, but there's no way in hell I'm going to wait an hour."

"You'll fucking do what I say, Riot, or so help me god I will have your patch ripped away so fast your head will spin, you fucking understand me? We're a team. I should have never let you go off by yourself. You go in there, your dick half-cocked and your brain all full of some fucked-up sense of bravado and you'll get your head blown off. You're outnumbered. Just fucking wait, you understand me, goddammit?"

He was right. I knew it. I fucking hated it, but I knew it.

"Alright. Fucking hurry, brother," my voice cracked, my heart swelling with pain and worry and pure anxiety.

"Please."

"Sit tight, brother. We're gonna get your girl."

TWENTY-NINE

Lacey

Slowly, I stood up, bringing myself to my full height, which wasn't much, but it still allowed me to tower over her, even as she stood in her four-inch heels.

"I thought I'd never see you again," I said, my voice calm, my heart exploding into painful pieces in my chest, as I looked down on the pathetic sack of flesh that brought me into this world.

"Oh, baby, you didn't really think that, did you?"

"Fuck yes I did," I said, resisting the urge to spit in her face.

She looked smaller than I remembered. Frail, almost.

I used to be so afraid of her, I thought. *Now, she looks like I could knock her over with one finger.*

"You changed your hair. It's not your color, you should change it back," she said, her hand reaching up to touch my hair.

I pushed her hand away before she made contact.

"I never abandoned you, Lacey."

"Like hell you didn't!" I said, my voice rising in anger. "Are you fucking delusional?"

"No, baby. I've been watching you the whole time, I was just staying out of the way."

My skin crawled.

"What the fuck do you mean? You *sold* me to Monty," I said, staring down at her.

"I didn't *sell* you to Monty. I just..well...*rented*...you to him."

"I don't understand. Do you even know what Monty did to me? He beat me. He raped me. Do you even care? He sold me to his fucking perverted friends, Mom. He traded me for money, power, used me as a pawn in whatever fucked up deal he had going on at the time."

"I know, baby," she said, shaking her head in disappointment. I was so confused.

"What do you mean you know?"

"I mean, I saw, like I said. I've been watching you. Trust me, Monty didn't make a move without consulting me first. I had him by the balls, and oh - nevermind!" she said, waving her hand dismissively. "We can talk about that later. Look - come! I have a present for you!"

She gestured to the bed, and I looked over at the clothes laid out on it. A short, red satin dress was spread across the orange flowered bedspread, the colors clashing so violently it was hard to look at. A pair of patent-leather red pumps sat to the right of the dress, with a set of black lace bra and panties laid out on the right.

"Do you like them?" she asked, her high-pitched, nasally voice raking across my brain. I walked over to the bed to get a closer look, looking for some clue of sanity in an undeniably insane situation. "You need to be dressed up for this."

"For this? For what? Seeing you?" I turned back to her, my eyes meeting hers angrily. "I hoped I'd never have to see you again. How did you even find me?" I asked.

"I never lost you. I knew you got arrested, so I waited at the police station to talk to Monty. He never showed up, but you came out, and I followed you. I already knew where you lived. So, I just waited to see what would happen. But Monty didn't come out for a long time, and when I saw you being whisked away by a bunch of strangers, I knew something was up. I followed you to where they turned off the road, and then I spent some time digging around the town. You'd be surprised what a washed up old lady can learn in a sleepy old town. Especially one that only has one nearby bar. People talk, baby."

"Whatever. You're fucking pathetic."

"Oh, baby, I know you're angry. I know you don't understand, but that's okay. You've always been a little stubborn, haven't you? I think you get that from me." She reached down, and picked up the dress from the bed. She outstretched her arms, and held it in front of my body. "I think it'll just fit. Your boobs have gotten bigger, haven't they? That's good, though, you were always a little too flat-chested. Men like a curvy woman, you know."

I snatched the dress from her hands, and threw it on the ground.

"You're fucking crazy, you know that? What kind of person does what you did to me? Not just the Monty shit, but all the shit before that, too? The pageants, the commercials, the endless auditions! I was just a kid! You never let me be a kid at all! Do you know how much shit I missed out on? Everything! Every fucking thing! All because of you! Because of your fucked up dreams that you pushed onto me when you couldn't reach them yourself. And then, when I got old enough and strong enough to say no to you, you dealt me the strongest blow! How could you sell me like that?"

"I didn't fucking sell you! I told you that - I —,"

"—you rented me? What the fuck does even mean?" I screamed.

"Look, you really think you want the truth? You think you're old enough now that you can just escape and start over? You're nothing without me, Lacey! Nothing, you understand?!" she was in my face, as much as she could be as I towered over her.

The two men were standing by the door, blocking any escape I might attempt, watching our fucked up scene play out in front of them, a look of shock on their faces.

"You want the truth, you little bitch?" she continued. "I gave you to Monty because I knew he could make more money off your sorry ass than I could. He had rich friends, I didn't. He lent you out to them, and he split the fee with me. Sure, he thought he was buying you fair and square, but after the first time, I went back to him, and...*renegotiated*...our agreement." She paused, her eyes peering into mine searchingly. "I blackmailed him. He gave me a cut of the profits, or I'd leak it to the press. He was about to run for Mayor, it was the last thing he could afford getting out about him, and he caved. It was quite easy, actually. I should have done it from the beginning, but it all worked out in the end."

"Oh, did it?" I asked, sarcastically. "For who? You? Monty? You certainly weren't concerned about me. Fuck you!"

"Oh, but, baby, don't you see? Everything I've ever done was for you! I only wanted the best for you, that's why I pushed you so hard. I knew you could be successful with Monty, that's why I sent you to live with him. I wanted you to be comfortable and live a life of luxury...the life I never had. I didn't want to see you struggle the way you made me struggle."

"Life of luxury? I made you struggle?! Are you out of your fucking mind? You turned me into a whore, Mom! A fucking whore!"

"Oh, baby, you are just looking at everything wrong. There's nothing wrong with a woman using her body to help her get through life."

My blood ran cold, and my fists clenched at my sides, the words scraping from my throat like they were clawing their way through the depths of all the pain I had stuffed away.

"I wasn't using my body, Mom. I was forced. I was raped! They took it all from me, Mom. You took it all from me."

"No, baby, you took it from me! Before I got pregnant with you, I was beautiful, I had a future. But no, your loser father knocked me up and left me and what was I stuck with? A crying baby, and a ruined body! My future flew out the window when you were born. You were my only hope, Lacey, don't you see? If I couldn't succeed with you, then I couldn't succeed. And then what did you do? You ungrateful little bitch, you just decide you can refuse to follow our dreams, just turn your back and decide you didn't want to do it anymore? You couldn't play by the rules, could you?"

"What rules, Mom? The rules of you constantly high on coke and blowing the judges to fix the pageants?"

"I was just trying to help. You threw it all away, Lacey. So, no, I didn't take anything from you - I did no such thing. I helped you. Just like I'm going to help you now, baby."

"You aren't doing a fucking thing to help me now, and you never have." My eyes trailed down to her throat, and the urge to wrap my fingers around it overwhelmed me.

"Oh, baby, yes I can! Monty's dead now! Well, of course you know that, don't you? I must admit, baby, I was a little surprised to learn you killed him. So violently, too! But the bastard deserved it, didn't he? He was a bit of prick, wasn't he? Waste of good pair of shoes, though," she said, her voice slicing through me. "Anyway, that's all water under the bridge, isn't it? The thing is...Monty and I had an agreement. If anything ever happened to him, you belong to me again."

I shook my head, the full realization of just how fucking crazy she really was finally dawning on me.

"You're insane," I whispered. "I'm free now. Free from you. Free from Monty...free from that fucking awful life that you condemned me to."

"No, baby, no....you see, that's not how this is going to work. I gave birth to you, Lacey. That counts. That counts big time. You can't just walk away from me. I own you. I'm your mother. I've always owned you. Not Monty. Me," she reached up to touch my face again, and I slapped her hand away harder this time.

"Don't fucking touch me!" I screamed, stepping away from her, my voice high and panicked.

"Lacey! You fucking listen to me, you little bitch!"

"Why should I?" I said, stepping back to her, leaning down, my face mere inches from hers. "You're a fucking pathetic mess. I'm not afraid of you anymore. I used to be, sure, but I'm bigger than you now. I'm older, I'm smarter. I don't have to put up with your shit…with anyone's shit. You have no fucking hold on me anymore, Mom." I shook my head. "Not Mom. Never Mom. I'm fucking out of here."

I turned toward the door, the two goons staring at us, both of them looking even more shocked at the ugly mother-daughter reunion.

"Lacey, you aren't going anywhere. Not yet." I heard the gun cock, and I turned back to see her pointing it straight at me. "Not till you put this dress on and then we are both going to present you with your new owner."

Her words stopped me in my tracks. I shook my head slowly, her intentions slowly sinking in.

"You were planning to sell me again?" I whispered incredulously.

"Well, like I said, not sell - just…rent," she winked playfully, the gun still pointed straight at me. She was so fucking lost in her own world, so far away from any normal sense of reality, that it was almost laughable. If it wasn't my fucking life we were talking about, that is. "I have a very wealthy man waiting at the Hilton that's shown some interest. But you have to look your best! Hey, remember when we put your hair up in a French braid for the Miss Teen Oregon pageant, and you had those little tendrils left hanging around your face? That was so classy, we should do that again."

She rambled on aimlessly, and the world began spinning around me.

Was this really happening? I looked at the door, still blocked by her men, whoever they were. *Bodyguards? Pimps? Were they planning on taking a turn with me, too?*

"No. I don't think so," I replied, shaking my head as I turned my gaze on the bed.

"Lacey, you will do as I say, or else!"

"Or else what? You're going to shoot me? You'd be destroying your meal ticket, if you did that, wouldn't you?" I asked, realizing she wouldn't dare shoot me, as I picked up the pair of red stilettos off the bed, and turned back to her.

"You'll do as I say, Lacey, or Ronnie and Eddie here will make you."

"Don't you understand, Mom?" I asked, closing the distance between us, the gun pressing against my chest, cold and hard. "Nobody makes me do anything any more. I'm not your little girl anymore."

I'm not sure what I was thinking, if I was thinking, if I was even capable of coherent thoughts at this point, but in a split second, my arm raised up, knocking the gun from her hand, and sinking the stiletto into her neck all in one smooth movement. Her eyes widened in surprise, and dark ribbons of blood began spurting out of her neck as I sank it in a second time and pulled it out again.

She fell to the ground, and I fell on top of her, my arm flailing, up and down, in and out, her neck and face slathered in thick, sticky, warm blood. The shoe fell from my hands, the heel almost broken off, dangling from the shoe like a broken limb. I picked up the other shoe from the ground where I had dropped it, and using all the force that my body would allow, stabbed it right into her eye.

"Stop fucking looking at me!" I screamed at her ugly dead eyes. "I fucking hate you! You ruined me!"

The words bubbled from me as I continued stabbing her, over and over as she lay dead below me.

"Fuck this shit, I'm outta here, man," one of the men at the door said.

"Yeah, I didn't sign up for a fucking murder," the other man snarled, turning to the door.

I didn't hear them.

I was still screaming. Still stabbing.

THIRTY

Riot

I paced the parking lot like a hungry lion. The hour passed by in a blur of frustration. By the time I felt the vibrating roar of the entire herd of the God's bikes approaching, I was wound up like a cobra ready to strike.

"Holy shit," Diana whispered as the Gods turned into the parking lot. "The cavalry has arrived."

"You'd best get in your car and get out of here," I said to her.

"Are you fucking kidding? This is the best break I've ever gotten on a story. I'm filming this shit," she said, pulling a camera from her trunk.

She had explained herself during the wait, told me how she had friends on the Portland police force, and that Grace was a kind of revered legend, the work she was doing, while still very hush-hush, was still whispered about. When Diana found out about the Mayor's slaying, and that a young woman was the suspect, she had ventured out to Tillamook on a hunch. A hunch that had paid off in a big way.

"I don't think so," Slade said, as he walked up to us, the first one off his bike.

"No filming during club business, miss," he smiled at her, using charm instead of force, just like he always did when he wanted a woman to do something. "Probably best you stay in the car, okay?"

And just like always, Diana fell for it. Her eyelashes fluttered, she began stuttering and she put her camera back in the trunk, walking to the side of the car as if in a trance.

I shook my head, and walked right over to Ryder, as Slade followed.

"They're in Room 117. It's been quiet so far. I can't see through the curtains, but the reporter says she's positive that's the room. The car's parked over there. Definitely not cops."

I didn't wait for him to reply, I just turned and started toward the door.

"Wait, Riot! Goddammit!"

I thundered back to him.

"I've waited long enough! It's time to fucking get in there, for fuck's sake!" I growled, not caring anymore that he was my President. All I cared about was Lacey. "What would you do if that was Grace in there?"

"I wouldn't let Grace get in that situation in the first place," he replied, his lips drawn tight and angry across his face.

"Yeah, well, not everyone is fucking perfect like you, Ryder. I fucked up, okay? I let her get under my skin, and now I'm paying for it, alright? Do you see me, man? Do you fucking see what I'm going through?" I yelled.

"Yeah, brother," Ryder replied, his eyes narrowing. "I see you. I get it, but we need a fucking plan first. You're not alone in this, Riot. We're a fucking brotherhood, or did you forget that?"

Slade, Zander, Doc, and Thorn stood behind Ryder, reminding me of who I was. He was right. He was always right. The man of few words, and yet, the best thoughts.

"Okay, man, you're right," I nodded.

"So, we're looking at two men for sure, and maybe more. Zander and Doc you go to the left side of the door, Thorn and I will go the right.

Riot, you knock, and don't stand in front of the fucking door, whatever you do. Slade, keep an eye on the other rooms and watch our backs. As soon as the door opens, we barrel in and take out anyone between us and Lacey."

I nodded, my body ready to come apart at the seams.

"Let's do this shit," Slade said.

We surrounded the door. Six guns cocked, drawn, ready to fire. As long as Lacey or one of my brothers didn't get hit, I didn't give a shit what happened to anyone.

I raised my fist to the door, and before I could knock, I heard Lacey's screams, and then the door opened.

The first man walked out, and Slade put a bullet in his head right away. He fell to the ground in a heap. His partner followed, with Zander's bullet slicing through his head, leaving a bloody trail on the door as he fell on top of the other guy.

I ran in the room, and stopped in my tracks.

Lacey was covered in blood, leaning over a woman's body, gripping a broken, bloody shoe, her arm flailing up and down, slicing into the woman over and over.

I ran to her, grabbed her, but she was frantic, hysterical. Her eyes were wild, and the Lacey I knew wasn't there. This was someone else, a wild animal trapped in a cage, clawing frantically as they tried to escape.

She swung at me but I ducked, the shoe slicing through the air over my head.

"Lacey!" I yelled, but she didn't stop. She was sobbing, screaming, her hands flailing in the air. I grabbed her arms, calling her name again, but she wrestled against me, lost in her own horrific nightmare.

I held her arms. She was strong, really strong, but I was stronger, and I held her arms down, her fist still clutching the broken shoe, as she tried to break free.

I gripped her tightly, and I did the only thing I could think of to do.

I kissed her.

I pressed my lips against her mouth firmly, roughly, silencing her screams. She fought against me, trying to push me away, but I held onto her arms, my lips still pressed to hers, until at last, she relaxed, the fight fading from her limbs, and I loosened my grip.

I pulled away, looking into her eyes.

"It's me, Lacey. It's Riot. You're safe now, sweetheart."

She looked up at me, her face streaked in blood, and she blinked hard, and shook her head. The darkness faded and the light returned to her eyes as she realized it was me.

The Lacey that I knew and loved had returned.

Loved.

The broken, bloody shoe fell to the ground and she wrapped her arms around me, crying, sobbing, her whole body shaking violently.

"It's over," she whispered through her tears. "It's really over…"

EPILOGUE

The Gods, Grace, Lacey, Cherry and Tiff huddled around the television set, all eyes and ears intently focused on the news.

"I'm Diana Trudeau, with KATU News."

The Gods began hooting and hollering, pushing Slade off the couch.

"There's your girlfriend, Slade," Thorn teased him.

"Shut the fuck up!" Slade growled, standing back up. "It was just one fucking night, and you've got us fucking married already!"

Slade and Diana had hooked up after meeting at the motel that day. After all the shit that went down, Slade invited her to come back to the clubhouse. Half to make sure that what she was going to be reporting wouldn't jeopardize Solid Ground at all, and half to see what she was like in bed. He had succeeded on both counts.

"Today, police reported that former Mayor of Seattle, Monty Patterson, has been implicated in a string of sex-trafficking operations throughout the West coast. The woman police were looking for earlier, Lacey Carrington, has been questioned and released. Sources say Ms. Carrington confessed to killing Mayor Patterson in self-defense, and the DA has declined to press charges or comment on the case any further. Reporting from Portland, I'm Diana Trudeau."

Ryder turned off the television.

"And, that's that. Good job, Slade," Grace said.

"I aim to please," he said, arrogantly throwing his arms behind his head, and his feet up on the coffee table. "Haven't had a woman complain yet."

"Oh, please," Riot said, his arm thrown around Lacey's shoulders as she leaned her head on his shoulder. "You wouldn't hear them if they did, you've got your head so far up your own ass."

"Fuck you, Riot, don't make me embarrass you in front of your girl," Slade replied. "You're due for a beat down."

Two weeks had passed since Lacey had killed her mother and collapsed in Riot's arms. They had been inseparable since then. Lacey had been badly shaken, spending most of her days and nights recovering in Riot's bedroom, but she was starting to come around again and return to her usual self, and slowly opening up to her new family. The envelope with her new identity lay unopened in her room.

A grand jury had decided against indicting her on either Monty's death or her mother's, writing them both off as self-defense. The other two guys the Gods shot were chalked up to being in the wrong place at the wrong time. The cops were being generous as a favor to Grace.

"Yeah, sure, bro, whatever," Riot replied to Slade. He turned to Lacey, his eyes lighting up every time he looked at her. "Let's go for our walk, babe."

Hand in hand they walked out into the darkness of the Tillamook forest, their steps falling into sync, the warmth of their bodies as close as they could get.

Their nightly walks had become expected, quickly becoming a ritualistic study in the constantly changing dynamics of a new relationship.

Riot had learned quickly. He could read Lacey easily, knowing when to fall back and let her lead, or when to grab her hand confidently and show her the way. Tonight, they followed a familiar trail side by side.

When they reached the creek, they hiked alongside it, climbing over rocks and ducking under fallen trees, until they reached Riot's private spot.

"I don't think I'll ever get tired of coming here," Lacey said, turning her smile up to her rock, her Riot, as he pulled her into his strong arms.

He leaned down, brushing his lips against hers, the heat rushing forth, his cock twitching in his pants, just like it did every time he touched her.

"I hope you never do," he replied.

"I don't think it's possible," she whispered.

The silent swoosh of two pairs of wings brushed past them. Oliver and Olivia landed on a wet rock beside them, patiently waiting for the affectionate petting that would surely come.

Lacey reached down, her fingers sliding through their feathers as they cooed and blinked at her.

"They're so beautiful," she whispered.

"So are you, Lacey," Riot said, his eyes tender and full of love.

"You are so kind to me, Riot," Lacey said, standing up and wrapping her arms around him. "I don't know what I ever did to deserve you."

"Don't you know, babe?" he asked, his gruff beard rubbing against her cheek as he pulled her in close.

"Nope," she replied, nestling into his body.

"Everybody deserves love like this. It was just meant to be. Everything you went through. Everything I went through. All the hell, the pain, the heartache, all the days of being lost in a sea of misery, it all led us here. To this moment, to this day, to this forest." He bent his head to kiss her, their lips melding together perfectly, and then he stomped on the ground, his black leather boots packing down the earth below it. "It all led to this solid ground beneath our feet. No more sea of misery, babe."

"Do you think it was all worth it?" she asked, pulling away slightly, staring back into his smiling eyes.

"If it means I get to spend the rest of my life with you, then yes."

Oliver and Olivia grew tired of watching them, their white spotted wings swooshing through the air as they took flight, leaving Riot and Lacey alone in the dark forest.

"I thought they'd never leave!" Riot said, as he pulled off his boots and ripped the shirt from his muscular torso. Lacey laughed, joining him, knowing exactly what was coming next.

"Race you to the waterfall!" he said, as he began running away from her.

The moonlight shone down on them, the sounds of the forest filtering through the trees, as they leaped over rocks and raced their way to the fall.

Riot always won this game, each time greeting Lacey wearing nothing but a smile and that thick, always present beard, the rest of his clothes discarded along the way.

"You always win!" she complained, as he took her into his arms again, his cock hard and throbbing between them.

"I know," he laughed. "And look at my prize…"

Their heads bent together, their gentle kisses turning passionate, as the roar of the waterfall behind them drowned out the songs of their lovemaking, the misty water clinging to their hair, the pain of their pasts drifting away like a fallen leaf being carried away on the surface of the water.

THE END

ABOUT THE AUTHOR

Honey Palomino is a true romantic at heart!

She loves reading and writing about dangerously sexy bad boys and the women that love them!

OTHER TITLES BY HONEY PALOMINO

MOTORCYCLE CLUB ROMANCE

Gods of Chaos Motorcycle Club

Outlaws Motorcycle Club

Dirty Crow Motorcycle Club

Captured

Old_Ghosts

Saving Rebel

Jett

My Brother's Keeper

BAD BOY BILLIONAIRE ROMANCE

The Crown Jewels

BAD BOY COWBOY ROMANCE

Hope Against Hope

Abandon All Hope

Hope Springs Eternal

Made in the USA
Las Vegas, NV
25 August 2021